IMPOSSIBLE TALES

To Sophie,

Anything is possible!

D. Worsley

Dan Worsley

Text copyright © Dan Worsley 2016
Cover and interior illustrations copyright
© Martin Spore 2016
All rights reserved

Dan Worsley and Martin Spore assert the moral
right to be identified respectively as the author
and illustrator of this work.

This book is entirely a work of fiction.
Names, characters, businesses, places, events and
incidents are all used in a fictitious manner.
Any resemblance to actual persons, living or
dead, or actual events is purely coincidental.

No part of this book may be used or reproduced
in any manner whatsoever without written
permission from the author, except in the case of
brief quotations embodied in critical articles for
review purposes.

ISBN: 978-1530999996

Also by Dan Worsley:

*To Clancy, for backing me from
the start and helping me to prove
that anything is possible*

Contents

Keep Your Hair On

Dad inspected his daughter's long blonde locks. "Your hair's desperate for a cut," he said.

Alicia's face lit up. "Let's head into town," she said excitedly. "I love going to the hairdressers. It's been ages since I last went. Come on, Dad."

"That's the problem. Money's tight at the minute and haircuts don't come cheap," Dad explained as he rummaged around in the kitchen drawer. "I reckon I could do it with these," he said, brandishing a pair of kitchen scissors which he'd found amid the clutter.

"I'm not sure," Alicia nervously replied, warily eyeing the scissors. "Do you know what you're doing?"

Dad ushered Alicia towards a chair, sat her down and studied her hair like a painter about to begin work on a fresh canvas. "Yeah, how difficult can it be?" he asked.

After a hesitant start, Dad's confidence grew and in turn, more and more of Alicia's blonde locks began to cascade like a golden waterfall. A pile of hair was quickly building on the faded lino.

"How's it looking, Dad?" Alicia asked nervously.

"Really good," Dad replied, failing to give his daughter a true picture of the destruction which was taking place. "I think it needs to be a bit shorter."

"Not too short, please," Alicia replied.

Unfortunately, Dad wasn't listening. He was so carried away with his chopping and cutting that he was in his own little world. Blonde strands and straggly clumps dropped to the floor, adding to the rapidly growing mass of cut hair.

Dad stepped back to view his handiwork. The realisation of what he'd done hit him like a knockout blow from a heavyweight boxer. Alicia's hair now resembled an explosion in a spaghetti factory! Blonde strands of differing lengths stuck out here and there. The more the desperate man had tried to correct his initial errors, the worse the situation had become. Moving round so that he faced his daughter, who remained blissfully unaware of what was happening, he started work on her fringe.

It began to dawn on Dad that things were lurching from bad to worse and his hands trembled. The scissors jumped around and hacked chunks out of what a few minutes earlier had been a ruler-straight fringe.

Sensing things were going badly wrong, Alicia instructed her father to stop. She leapt from the kitchen chair and stepped back to survey the scene of carnage. Clumps and long strands of hair littered the kitchen floor. She raised her hands to her head and ran her fingers through her butchered locks. Tears welled in her eyes.

"I think I can even it up," said Dad, struggling to believe his own words.

"Even it up? Even it up? You aren't going anywhere near it!" Alicia screeched as she made a dash for the bathroom mirror to fully inspect the damage.

As Alicia looked at her reflection, the seriousness of the situation struck her like a juggernaut. Her beautiful long blonde hair had been destroyed. How could she go to school looking like this? The other children would taunt her. Alicia slumped to her knees and tears cascaded down her freckled cheeks. Dad had single-handedly ruined her life!

Leaving his daughter to calm down, Dad sat in his armchair and placed his head in his hands before sighing deeply. He knew his daughter's hair was beyond repair and he didn't have the cash to put things right. Dad thought his day couldn't go any further downhill. Little did he know things were about to lurch from bad to worse.

Suddenly, deafening music began to thump and thud through the partition wall which separated Dad and Alicia's flat from their awful neighbour.

Mr Spitt was a thug of a man. He'd made their life hell since he'd moved in a few months earlier. His incessant, thumping dance music, which blasted out at all times of day and night, had nearly pushed Dad and Alicia over the edge.

Dad leant over and banged his fist three times on the floral wallpaper. Rather than turning the music down, the odious Mr Spitt thumped the wall in reply before turning up the volume to an ear-splitting level. The ornaments on the windowsill were now jiggling around. Dad shook his head and got up from his chair. He hated confrontations, so going round to complain face to face wasn't an option. Complaining to the council seemed like a sure-fire way of poking the hornets' nest as it would only make the situation even more unbearable.

As Dad stood with his hands over his ears, Alicia appeared from the bathroom, also shielding her ears from the deafening racket. She signalled towards the front door before moving to the coat stand and picking up a beanie hat which she pulled over her butchered locks. Opening the front door, Alicia walked out with

Dad close behind. They headed down the communal stairs and outside into the warm sunshine to seek some much-needed peace and quiet.

After walking in silence for a couple of minutes, Alicia finally broke the deadlock. "I don't know which I hate most, my haircut or our vile neighbour. They're both sickening in their own way."

"I'm so sorry," replied Dad, gently putting his hand on his daughter's shoulder. "I was trying my best."

Alicia halted her dad mid-apology and pointed to the shop which they were about to pass. The sign looked like it could fall down at any moment and the writing was faded and hard to read, but Alicia could just make out that it read 'Waldron's Wigs'.

"Can we have a look in?" she pleaded. "They might have something to cover up this mess until my hair grows back."

Before Dad could answer, Alicia was browsing the wide range of wigs and hairpieces on display. He stared around the shop, amazed at the vast array of items on offer. There were long black wigs, bobbed ginger ones and wigs for men too.

"We've wigs to suit all budgets," said a tall lady wearing a flowery dress. She frowned as she inspected Alicia's massacred mullet. "You're not the first person to come in for a cover-up wig after a home-haircut disaster, let me tell you."

"We're shopping on a budget," said Dad. "Money's tight at the minute. If I'm completely honest, we're broke."

"Hmmm, I think I may have just the thing," advised the lady as she pushed her way through a curtain at the back of the shop.

"I don't want to look like a complete freak with some dodgy wig," Alicia hissed.

Before Dad could reply, the lady returned with a wig made from long blonde hair. It looked remarkably natural and very much like Alicia's real hair had done before Dad had been let loose with the scissors.

"Would you like to try it on? I think it'd be perfect and well within your budget," said the shop owner.

"Please," replied Alicia as she turned round to allow the lady to fit the wig.

After a few minor adjustments, Alicia's hair was hidden away and she stared into a mirror to admire the false locks.

"Can I ask how much this wig is?" enquired Dad, clearly sweating over the price.

"You can have it for free," replied the shop owner with a smile. "This wig is actually second-hand and for that reason, people don't seem keen to buy it. If I can make this little girl happy by giving it to you, then so be it."

"I'm not bothered that it's second-hand. Thank you very much," said Alicia as she continued to admire herself in the mirror.

"There's one more thing," added the shop owner. "The wig belonged to a lady who died while wearing it. I've got to tell you that. I know some people are a bit squeamish about such minor details."

Pulling the wig off, Alicia squealed and held it at arm's length. "She popped her clogs with this wig on her head?" she yelled.

"Yes, that's correct my dear," said the shop owner. "It's been thoroughly washed and cleaned. I'm afraid it's that or nothing as the rest are clearly out of your price range."

Alicia thought carefully while inspecting the wig. She was in a no-win situation. She either had to run the gauntlet of the other kids when she returned to school with her current 'haircut' or it could be disguised with a dead woman's wig.

"Thanks. We'll take it," Alicia said, as Dad nodded in agreement.

The shop owner smiled before refitting the wig.

"It looks exactly like your hair," said Dad. "Give it a couple of weeks and I'll save up for a professional haircut. It's only a short-term solution."

As they headed home, Alicia felt comfortable again.

The wig disguised the abomination underneath. In a couple of weeks, everything would get back to normal. How could anything possibly go wrong?

* * *

When Monday morning finally came, Alicia made sure that she was up early to sort out her wig. She didn't want anyone at school spotting the difference and decided it'd be best kept a secret. After carrying out a final check, she headed off to school where the morning passed without event. Unfortunately, everything changed during a visit to the toilets at the beginning of lunch.

Alicia adjusted the wig in the only mirror which hadn't been vandalised and turned to leave the toilet. The door suddenly swung open and in walked Veronica, the one person she was desperate to avoid. This girl had a track record for making Alicia's life difficult.

"Just the person I was after," grunted Veronica. "I'm sure I saw you and your old man going into that dump of a wig shop on Saturday."

Alicia's blood ran cold. The last person she wanted to know about her haircut disaster was the school bully! She'd never hear the last of it. Veronica would make her life hell.

"Er…no. I was away all weekend visiting my aunt,"

Alicia replied in a thinly disguised lie which she hoped Veronica wouldn't unpick.

"Really? There aren't many little freaks like you knocking about this town. Plus, your aunt died last year, I remember you being off school to go to the funeral. I had to last for two whole days without giving you a dead arm," said Veronica. "It was torture!"

Alicia gulped. She'd been rumbled. Fear coursed through her body. Her gut twisted into a knot and it felt like an invisible hand was gripping her throat, preventing any words from escaping. Lying to Veronica wasn't advisable and usually resulted in some form of punishment.

"You know how I deal with little liars," growled a clearly angry Veronica. She grabbed Alicia's arm tightly and drew back her fist. Alicia closed her eyes. Tears splurged down her cheeks as she braced herself for the imminent pain.

Rather than feeling the impact on her arm, Alicia sensed movement on her head. Before she could react, she heard an ear-piercing scream. She opened her eyes and struggled to take in what she was seeing.

On the floor, writhing and thrashing around, Veronica was wrestling with the blonde wig. The squirming hairpiece was viciously attacking the girl. Veronica was yelping and screaming, probably as much in shock as in pain. The blonde wig was pulling at

Veronica's ginger hair and yanking at her ears. The desperate girl was rolling over and over on the floor, frantically clawing at the wig as she tried to fight it off.

Alicia stared in disbelief as Veronica begged for mercy, her words barely audible as she cried hysterically and snivelled like a baby. "Stop!" screamed Alicia. The wig automatically halted its onslaught and scuttled across the tiled floor. It slithered up the pipes to the sink before launching itself into the air and landing on Alicia's head. It quickly rearranged itself with a little assistance from its owner.

Veronica pushed herself backwards across the floor and sat with her back against the wall. Her eyes were wide with terror and she was staring at the blonde wig which had only seconds earlier been mercilessly attacking her. "That thing's deadly! It tried to kill me. You made it attack me," she babbled incoherently. "Just wait until I tell Mr Longbottom. He'll take it off you and everyone will laugh at your shocking haircut."

"And you think people are going to believe a crazy tale about a wig which came to life and attacked you? I think there's more chance they'll call your parents and advise them to take you to see a doctor. Everyone will think you've lost your mind. Now get out of here!" said Alicia with a newly found confidence.

Veronica wiped away a long string of snot dribbling from her nostrils and clambered to her feet. Her eyes remained firmly locked on the blonde wig which was now innocently perched on Alicia's head. Grabbing the handle, she opened the door and dashed out.

Alicia reached up and felt the synthetic strands of hair, then shook her head in puzzled confusion. How could a wig come to life? Would it attack her? Pondering over those questions and many others, she wandered out into the corridor and headed to lunch.

The afternoon was trouble-free and the wig behaved itself perfectly. Before she knew it, Alicia was walking home and considering whether to tell her dad about the incident. She was pretty sure that Veronica would keep quiet about it for fear of being labelled a liar or worse.

Alicia cut through the back alley which led to the block of flats. She could already hear the thumping bass of the non-stop dance music that was pumping out of the open windows of Spitt's flat. Her heart sank. The situation was making both her and Dad miserable.

As she pulled out her door key, she froze in her tracks. About ten metres ahead of her, a huge black dog growled aggressively in her direction. Alicia's feet felt like they were glued to the floor. Her heart hammered against her ribcage. She prayed the dog would leave her alone and head off in another direction. Unfortunately, it continued to bare its teeth and growl at her. It didn't seem to have an owner close by and she didn't recognise it as one of the regular mutts which roamed the streets around the flats.

She slowly moved backwards, praying that the dog would lose interest, but instead it began to prowl towards her. It barked ferociously and she could see its sharp teeth coated in drool.

The poor girl's heart was thundering and a surge of adrenaline caused her to turn and run. The dog pelted along after her, its paws pounding on the tarmac. She could hear its barking getting louder as it gained on her. She risked a look over her shoulder; the creature was bounding closer and closer.

The wig began to wriggle and jiggle. It squirmed around on Alicia's head before launching itself into the air, landing between Alicia and the dog. The startled beast skidded to a halt and snapped and growled at the wig, which was now scuttling in its direction.

In one swift movement, the wig leapt up onto the dog's head, wrapping itself around the beast and bringing it to the floor. The dog rolled and writhed as it desperately pawed at the wig.

"Enough! Stop!" yelled Alicia as the dog howled like a puppy, clearly no longer a threat. The wig released its grip on the befuddled pooch and the beast ran away with its tail between its legs.

The wig scurried towards Alicia, who was kneeling on the tarmac. It proceeded to whirl like a cyclone before twirling up into the air and landing back on the young girl's head. Within a few seconds it was back in position.

Alicia sat on the pavement and gathered her thoughts. Twice that day the wig had come to her rescue. It sounded like a bizarre theory, but it seemed that as well as covering up her horrendous haircut, it had assumed the role of chief protector. Alicia stood up and decided to head home to explain the day's events to Dad.

As usual, the lift wasn't working so she trudged up the six flights of stairs to get to the flat. Mr Spitt's thumping music was getting louder. All she wanted was some peace and quiet, but that didn't seem likely any time soon.

As she turned the corner into the corridor which led to the flat, Alicia saw two men. As she got closer, she realised that one was Dad and the other was Mr Spitt. Their nasty neighbour was pushing Dad against the wall. Out of nowhere, Spitt drew back his other fist and thumped Dad in the stomach. Alicia gasped as the poor man's knees buckled and he sagged to the floor.

"Hey! Leave my dad alone!" yelled Alicia as she ran down the corridor.

"And what'll you do if I don't, little girl?" mocked Mr Spitt. Dad was lying on the floor in a crumpled heap, moaning and groaning. "I'll play my music as loud as I want and you and your loser dad won't stop me. He knows what'll happen if he complains again."

Alicia was terrified. Her heart thundered and she felt physically sick. This man was a thug. He was completely unpredictable and if he was willing to assault Dad in broad daylight, he was capable of anything.

As if it sensed her fear, the wig began to stir. The strands of hair began to twist and twirl causing the thug to stare open-mouthed at Alicia's head. Suddenly, the wig hurled itself across the corridor and latched on to Spitt's head. It covered his face, causing the man to blindly stagger around. Dad stared aghast at what he was seeing. Alicia, on the other hand, wore a grin from ear to ear, resisting the temptation to call off the attack. Mr Spitt let out muffled cries as he flopped to his knees, still battling with the wig which was now torturing him by yanking out the hairs from up his nose.

"He's had enough now," Alicia reluctantly said. The wig obediently followed the call of its master and left the bewildered man in a quivering heap on the floor. It slithered along the carpet before climbing up Alicia's body and resetting itself on her head. At that second the door at the end of the corridor opened and a police officer appeared. He moved briskly towards the trio.

"That kid's wig attacked me," wailed Mr Spitt as he

cowered against the wall. "It was trying to kill me! Please help me, officer. Arrest her for assault."

Trying to mask his amusement, the policeman placed a hand on Spitt's shoulder and hauled him to his feet. "You can tell me all about that nasty killer wig down at the station," said the officer in a mocking tone. "I'd also like to hear about the incident involving Mr Atkins. One of the other residents informed us an assault was taking place."

He handcuffed the bewildered thug and read him his rights before leading him away. Alicia helped Dad to his feet and the pair headed into the flat.

"You shouldn't have got involved out there. You could've been badly hurt by that brute," Dad ranted, suspiciously eyeing the blonde wig.

"Keep your hair on, Dad," replied Alicia. "I'll stick the kettle on, then I'll tell you everything."

Life for Alicia and Dad was much improved from that day. Mr Spitt was charged with assaulting Dad and refused to return to his flat for fear of another wig attack. The council moved him elsewhere and confiscated his stereo and speakers. As for Alicia, she finally got her long-awaited haircut a few weeks later. She ended up keeping hold of the wig though. She had a feeling that one day it would come in useful again.

Fear Of The Unknown

Lightning illuminated the pitch-black night sky. Deafening thunder noisily rumbled and crashed. Down below, the sea was a boiling cauldron. The vicious waves raged, battering a helpless boat and causing the vessel to pitch and tip. The captain sent out desperate Mayday calls while the rest of the crew frantically battled to save the boat. One way or another, the merciless sea was going to devour its prey. It was simply a matter of time before the boat was dragged down to a watery graveyard.

Out on deck, a small wooden crate chained down at the rear of the boat broke free from its shackles. It began to slide sideways before colliding with the metal guardrail. The crate splintered, leaving a long crack down one side. From the darkness within the crate, a high-pitched shriek emerged before a glowing red eye stared out through the splintered wood, taking in the stormy chaos.

The captive within the crate was desperate to escape. It'd been caught in the trawler's nets and the fishermen had hauled it up from the depths. Believing their mysterious catch would command a good price at the fish market, they loaded it into the wooden crate and nailed it shut.

Out on deck, a terrified crew member made his way over to secure the prized catch as the unrelenting sea battered him. The waves clawed at his sodden clothes and did all they could to knock him off his feet. Eventually they succeeded.

The man staggered as the boat pitched violently. His arms flailed as he tried to grab the metal guardrail. His numb hands clutched at thin air and his rubber boots squeaked and slipped before he tumbled backwards over the side of the stricken vessel. Swallowing up the poor sailor and dragging him to his death, the waves returned for more, determined to satisfy their ravenous hunger. All of the time, the blazing red eye peered out of the crate, awaiting its opportunity to finally break free.

As the boat pitched hard to the left, the crate smashed against the metal rail again. This time the narrow crack became a gaping hole and the captive inside seized its opportunity. Pushing its long body through the gap, the creature slithered out of the crate. Its snake-like tentacles pulled its long body along the deck. With one swift slithering movement, it hauled itself up over the guardrail and plunged into the sea, disappearing below the frothing, frenzied waves.

* * *

The sun was setting and darkness was beginning to fall at Nexton-on-Sea. The beach was deserted as the visitors had long gone. They'd packed up their towels and picnic baskets and headed home, taking with them memories which would be treasured forever. Unfortunately, they'd left behind vast amounts of litter. Although the small seaside town welcomed visitors from far and wide, the piles of trash which they left in their wake were a major issue.

Suddenly, a ripple appeared in the dead-calm sea. A swirl on the surface followed, hinting that something below was on the move. The ripples headed towards the beach and large clusters of bubbles broke the surface.

A long tentacle poked out of the water, appearing to sample the view like a periscope being raised from a submarine. After momentarily taking in its new surroundings, the creature left the safety of the water, satisfied that it could take shelter without threat of being captured again.

It slithered across the golden sand, surveying the litter with blazing red eyes which glowed like flames. Lowering its head, it began to suck and slurp. It swallowed mouthful after mouthful of garbage from the beach. Cans and crisp packets disappeared into the cavernous opening. Leftover food and plastic bottles were vacuumed up. Before long the beach, which only minutes earlier had been an eyesore, was transformed into a beautiful stretch of golden sand.

Sensing movement in the distance, the creature spotted a deep pool of water under the pier which stretched out from the seafront. Slithering and sliding its way over, the creature submerged itself in the salty pool. It sank to the bottom, hopeful that it'd found a safe haven where it could live in peace.

After resting its weary body for a short while, the creature peered out from its watery hiding place. It sensed that the veil of darkness which had fallen was enough to protect it from human eyes. In addition, a thick fog had moved in off the sea and enveloped the beach and swallowed up the seafront. The darkness and the fog were a perfect combination. The creature cautiously slithered out of the pool and moved up the beach, before turning to peer out to sea through the dense gloom.

Its red eyes identified a set of lights in the distance. It was a freighter, larger than the fishing trawler which had been transporting the creature before the storm struck. The ship was moving at a startling rate of knots and heading directly towards the beach. Sensing imminent danger, and in an act of kindness which didn't match the way the creature had been treated by the fishermen, it decided to help. It began to shake and jiggle, its whole body convulsed and thrashed. The violent, jerking movements seemed to super-charge its large red glowing eyes which began to emit bright laser beams. They cut through the fog and darkness like hot knives through butter and initially dazzled the captain, who realised how close to danger he was.

Taking evasive action, the man began to change the boat's course and it veered away from the coastline which had threatened to beach it. The creature watched as the ship moved away and continued to shine its laser eyes until the vessel was no longer in sight. This mysterious creature had gone out of its way to perform an act of kindness which had undoubtedly averted a catastrophe.

After further exploration of the beach, the creature returned to its pool under the pier. It was satisfied with its helpful actions and it drifted off to sleep on the silt bed. In the depths of its hideout, it felt a contentment which it hadn't experienced before. Maybe the humans weren't the enemy after all.

Happy in its new home, the creature soon settled

into a routine. It would sleep at the bottom of the pool under the pier during the day. At night, under the cover of darkness, it would firstly clear the sands of the junk and debris left behind by the tourists, before patrolling the beach to ensure passing boats were kept safe. The creature was happy and contented with its new-found role. Little did it realise that one act of kindness would change everything forever.

* * *

The creature awoke that fateful morning to find its watery hidey-hole had been swallowed up by the incoming tide. Cautiously swimming out into open water, the nerves in the creature's skin tingled and buzzed as it sensed movement. Its glowing red eyes scanned the crystal-clear water and it identified the outline of a small human.

The boy's arms thrashed and his legs kicked as he fought with all his might to keep his head above water. Like a cork bobbing up and down, his head ducked under the waves and his attempts to stay afloat grew even more desperate. But the child was tiring and his legs were becoming heavy. The undercurrent which had dragged him away from the shallows was merciless in its attempts to drown him. Further and further out it hauled his weary body, making his cries for help no more than whispers on the wind.

The creature watched as the child's movements slowed and he began to sink. Moving closer, it wrapped its snake-like tentacles around his legs. Using all its energy, it forced the drowning child to the surface. The child's initial reaction was to gasp and gulp in life-saving air, but his relief quickly turned to panic. He realised that below the surface, something had hold of his legs. Terrified and disorientated, he began to scream and thrash his arms wildly.

The creature powered itself through the water; the child's saviour pushing him to shore. Flicking and twirling its tentacles, the beast neared the beach before launching the boy forward like a human missile. Swiftly retreating into the depths, so as not to alert the humans who were gathering on the beach, the creature watched from a safe distance. It saw the child crawling from the shallows on his hands and knees before sprawling on the beach, coughing and spluttering but very much alive. Returning to the safety of its watery hideout, the creature settled once again, unaware that its kind-hearted actions would eventually have devastating consequences.

* * *

"Order! Order!" called out a smartly dressed man wearing a black-rimmed pair of spectacles and a colourful bow tie. "We're here today to discuss the events which took place down…"

"That thing could've killed my lad," interrupted a tall man from the back of the meeting hall. "It's lucky he fought it off and got back to shore."

"I saw it under the water," yelled a woman. "It was chasing the poor kid. I think it was trying to eat him. Whatever it is, it's a killer!"

Trying to restore some order, the bespectacled man started to speak again. "But there are some reports saying that whatever it was actually helped the boy and saved his life. It pushed him ashore according to some folk."

"Rubbish! It was hunting him down. It grabbed his legs! We need to deal with it. We can't have something lurking in the sea. It'll scare off the visitors. It's only a matter of time before it drags someone under," ranted another man, his voice straining with anger and emotion.

"We need to take the boats out and see what we can find," suggested a woman. "If we find it, we can scare it off. We can drive it back out to sea and it'll go back to wherever it came from. If it doesn't, we'll kill it."

The audience began to clap and cheer. An explosion of excited voices erupted from the crowded room in support of the woman's suggestion.

"If that's what you all want, then that's what we'll do," replied the man in the glasses, happy to do anything which would prevent a possible riot. "High tide's 7am tomorrow so we'll meet at the seafront. All welcome. We can't have some unknown beast in our waters, I agree. We'll do as you've suggested!"

The locals cheered and hollered. Sadly, their misinformed decision would have terrible consequences for the town of Nexton-on-Sea.

* * *

The townsfolk flocked to the beach the next morning and clambered aboard the assembled vessels. The boats were launched and outboard motors roared and hummed. The water frothed and foamed. Voices boomed and thundered as the flotilla cruised out in a long line stretching from the pier to the other end of the beach. Some people were hanging over the sides, slapping the water with paddles, while others blindly jabbed with poles and pieces of wood.

The creature stirred. Its body sensed the vibrations passing through the water. It tensed. It listened. Cautiously surfacing, it could make out the humans on board their boats. It could see their twisted, angry faces and it didn't understand what was happening. Ever since it had found its way to Nexton-on-Sea, it had tried to avoid the humans while helping them in any way it could. Why were they behaving like this? What had it done wrong?

"It's there!" shrieked a bearded man who'd spotted the silhouette. He was jabbing an outstretched finger towards the pier. The boats began to change direction. "Get it!" he bellowed.

Terrified and fearing the prospect of capture yet again, the creature began to swim out into deeper water. Its heart pounded and fear flooded its body. The beast used its tentacles to power itself along. But it was no match for the humans and their speedy crafts which were gaining on it by the second. Still they slapped the water and noisily splashed, sending waves of vibrations through the poor creature's body. It had no option but to dive deeper and deeper and swim faster and faster. The light above began to fade and the creature entered a world of darkness.

Back on the boats, the townsfolk were jubilant. They'd successfully driven the creature away and, in their eyes, made their town safe once more. Some gave out high-fives while others jigged about, whooping and hollering. They turned the boats around and headed back to shore.

* * *

After their initial delight had died down, the folk of Nexton-on-Sea realised that driving the creature away had been a huge mistake.

Over the next few weeks, countless numbers of

swimmers got into difficulties in the unpredictable waters off Nexton-on-Sea. Fortunately, they all escaped with their lives, but it seemed only a matter of time before someone wouldn't be as lucky.

Litter began to build up on the beach, to such an extent that visitors decided to stay away and the sands became a no-go zone. Nobody wanted to spend their holiday sunbathing amid piles of discarded junk. Before long, the previously bustling streets of Nexton-on-Sea were deserted. The place became a virtual ghost town as the tourists decided to go elsewhere.

To compound the locals' woes, a boat lost in a thick blanket of fog ran aground, causing a catastrophic oil spillage. Wildlife for miles around was affected and as a result of the disaster many sea creatures died.

Every day, the townsfolk deeply regretted their decision to drive out the creature. The locals looked out to sea, silently pleading for the creature to return, but sadly it was never seen again.

The creature's legacy did live on, however. After another public meeting, it was decided that the residents needed to take drastic action if they were to save their town. They formed a community group, with all of the members determined to help out.

Each day the townsfolk organised themselves into teams and patrolled the beach, collecting junk and emptying the new bins which had been fitted to solve the litter problem. Some of the locals spent their time watching out for swimmers in distress and successfully rescued a number of people who might otherwise have died. At night they lit blazing beacons along the beach to warn off any boats which ventured too close to shore. After a short while, the place was transformed into a thriving seaside resort again and even though the creature didn't return, its short stay had left a permanent imprint on the town.

Ultimately, the residents of Nexton-on-Sea were left to rue their misguided choice to chase the creature away. They cursed their decision every day and it just made them realise that they really didn't know what they had until it was too late.

Hot-Shot Snot

Can you imagine how it feels to be allergic to everything? Some people get the sniffles when they go near animals, others sneeze and cough in the summer when there's pollen about. I used to be envious of folk like that. They should've tried being me. My eyes used to stream if I even saw a cat, let alone stroked it. Dust made me cough and wheeze, making me feel like a belt was being tightened around my chest. Washing powder would bring me out in a bright red rash. The list just went on and on. You name it and I had an allergy to it. But things dramatically improved a few years ago after a trip to the doctors. In fact, my life was never quite the same again.

* * *

"Oh you poor thing," Mum said, as I wiped away a long string of snot which was snaking its way out of my left nostril. "I can't stand to see you suffer. I'm sure Dr Yew will be able to help."

I nodded at Mum and forced a smile which was filled more with hope than expectation.

As we waited, I hoped and prayed that Dr Yew would come up with a miracle cure for my endless list of allergies. The supply of medicines I'd received over the years seemed to do very little to relieve the horrible symptoms. It seemed that I was allergic to life and nobody could do anything to help.

As I wiped away another tidal wave of mucus, my name appeared on the surgery monitor. Temporarily stemming the tide of sticky snot with a saturated tissue, I followed Mum into Dr Yew's room.

"Morning, Scott," said Dr Yew as I slumped down onto one of the chairs. "Oh dear, you look like you're suffering again. Let's see what we can do for you."

I nodded a silent reply as I rubbed at my itchy eyes which felt like someone had ground sand into them. I desperately struggled to resist the temptation to rub them again, as from past experience I knew it would only make things worse. Salty tears streamed down my cheeks and dripped off my chin. If I looked half as rough as I felt, I must have resembled a human wreck!

"I know we've tried every medicine going," said Mum, "but is there anything at all left? I can't stand to see him suffer like this. It's making his life an absolute misery."

Dr Yew removed her glasses and placed them on the desk. She frowned as she pondered the situation. "There's one last possibility. I don't want to get your hopes up as the treatment is at an early stage, but it seems that it may be useful to people with severe allergies, like Scott. I'd be willing to allow him to trial it. There's a possibility of side effects though, as with all medicines. They should only be minor, but you know where I am if you need to report anything."

"We'll try anything, Doctor. The poor kid's suffering. If it gives him a bit of relief it's got to be worth a shot," said Mum.

I nodded in agreement, determined not to get my hopes up after countless disappointments in the past.

Doctor Yew looked at me. "Right then, I think we'll give it a go. Pull up your right sleeve and I'll give you a single dose," she said.

I did as I was told and watched anxiously as she removed a small syringe from a refrigerator at the back of the room. She took off the cap from the needle before wiping my arm with a sterile swab.

"Sharp prick," she said as I looked away and focused on the poster hanging on the back of the door. "All done," she said within seconds, leaving me rather relieved that I'd felt little more than a scratch.

"Thanks, Doctor," said Mum. "I'll keep a close eye on him and I'll be in touch if we notice any problems."

"Perfect," said Dr Yew as she handed Mum a leaflet. "If you notice anything out of the ordinary just get in touch. You know where I am."

As we walked home, I realised that I hadn't needed to blow my nose for at least ten minutes and my eyes felt much more comfortable. This was massive progress.

Over the next few days, my symptoms seemed to dramatically clear up. My itchy, red eyes settled down and my chest didn't feel half as tight. Everything was working out perfectly! That was until a few days later when some seriously weird stuff started to happen.

* * *

As I was lounging on my bed watching TV, my nose began to tingle. Not the outside, it was high up inside my right nostril. It was the sort of itch that drives you mad and you desperately need to deal with straight away. So in the comfort and privacy of my own bedroom, I decided to do just that. I carefully slid a finger up my right nostril and wiggled it around. I rooted and rummaged. I delved and dug. The relief was instant and incredible. It was heavenly!

As I slowly withdrew my finger, I looked down to see a long string of yellow snot connected to my nail. It was hanging like a washing line and was still attached at some point up my nostril. I tugged the line of mucus and it stretched like an elastic band. With my other hand, I plucked it like a guitar string and it wobbled, sending tingling vibrations racing up my nose. My eyes watered and my face scrunched up. This was bizarre! I'm as partial to picking my nose as the next man, but never in all the years of bogey hunting had anything like this happened. Separating the rubbery snot from my fingernail, I allowed it to dangle from my nostril and tried to sniff it back up. It wobbled and jiggled, but rather than retracting it just continued to dangle like a long piece of snotty spaghetti.

I looked in the mirror to see the long yellow thread suspended from my nose, hanging well below my chin. It was like a yellow snake seeking a hiding place up the dark opening of my right nostril. What would people think if they saw me like this? I reached as far up my nostril as I could and took a firm grip of the snotty string. I yanked it quickly and the mucus snapped and dropped to the floor. In the mirror, I could see there was still a little bit of snot high up inside my nostril, but I figured it wouldn't be noticeable.

I picked up the string of snot and inspected it closely. The rubbery mucus seemed to glow and was covered with sparkling silver dots. On closer inspection, the snotty mass appeared to pulse and throb like it contained some sort of mystical energy source.

Let's be honest. Most people like to flick their bogies. It's a well-known fact. Well, I'm no different. I rolled up the string of snot between the fingers and thumb on my right hand. It felt squidgy and warm. I carefully formed it into a rubbery ball. Then I balanced it on my thumb before flicking it with my finger. The mucus missile hurtled at high speed towards the television. A yellow whizzing blur raced through the air, striking the TV screen and rebounding like a boomerang before returning to my hand. I couldn't believe what I'd seen. The force of the mucus projectile had pushed the TV back across the desk!

Taking aim again, I pinged the snot ball at an empty can on my bedside table. The snotty projectile struck the target like a bullet fired by a gunslinger, sending the can flying into the air. Yet again, the mucus ball whizzed back into my hand. My mind whirred. This was incredible! I was able to fire this strange snot like a stone from a catapult or a bullet from a gun.

I grinned to myself. I was no longer producing normal mucus. This stuff was hot-shot snot!

* * *

I decided it was best not to tell Mum about my mutated mucus. But I was desperate to share my news with someone. That's how I ended up sitting in the park with Frank, my best mate.

33

"I'm going to show you something, but I need you to keep it a secret," I said to Frank as he stretched out on the grass in the early morning sun.

"Yeah, no worries. Your secret's safe with me," he replied, shielding his eyes from the bright sunshine.

I pulled the yellow ball of snot from my trouser pocket, perched it on my thumb and scoured the park for a possible target.

"What on earth's that?" Frank asked, shooting me a quizzical look.

"It's snot, but not the normal stuff," I replied. "I pulled it from my nose yesterday. I reckon the medicine the doctor gave me has done something weird to my body."

"Yuk! That's gross. I think it's done something strange to your brain if you think your snot's mutated!" he said sarcastically. He laughed out loud and shook his head.

Out in the middle of the lake, I spotted a 'No fishing' sign sticking out of the water. Bingo! Target located.

"Keep your eyes on that sign," I told Frank, pointing at the wooden placard which was standing straight and true.

I closed one eye and took aim. Drawing back my finger, I flicked the yellow missile. It hurtled across the water and struck the sign with a thud, causing it to tilt.

Frank gasped and watched on, his mouth gaping open in shock. His eyes tried to follow the snot ball as it skimmed back over the water, but it was too fast.

"What just happened? How did you do that?" asked Frank in a stunned voice.

"I told you something weird was happening," I replied, "but I think it's best if we keep it quiet."

Frank nodded in silent agreement, still flabbergasted at what he'd witnessed.

Time was getting on and if we didn't get a move on we were going to be late for school. I stashed the snot in my pocket and we headed off.

* * *

The morning dragged. To be honest, I was delighted to hear the lunch bell which would give me an hour of freedom and the chance to examine the snot in more detail. Usually I'd have dreaded going out in the summer, but thanks to the new medicine, feeling the warmth of the sun on my face was now a pleasurable experience. I searched the yard for Frank, but there was no sign of him. As I made my way round the back of the school building, I spotted my friend.

Frank was whimpering and pleading for mercy. He was pinned up against a wall by Bazza, the school thug. His foot soldiers scuttled around him like rats, egging on the bully and mercilessly mocking Frank.

"I want your dinner money," hissed Bazza as he tightened his grip around Frank's throat. Bazza's two sidekicks danced around gleefully as Frank searched his pockets for the cash.

"Put him down, now!" I shouted, causing a surprised Bazza to lower Frank to the ground.

"Well, well, well. It's snotty Scotty Stott," mocked Bazza. "It's unusual to see you out here. Are you sure there's not something you're allergic to?" His sidekicks laughed hysterically and pretended to sneeze and cough.

Bazza moved towards me menacingly, his two minions jeering and gesturing as they scurried along beside him.

"Stay back, I'm warning you," I said, as I slipped my hand into my trouser pocket.

"What you gonna do? Sneeze on us?" growled Bazza. A chorus of laughter burst forth from his mates.

I pulled out the yellow snot ball and perched it on my thumb. The trio stopped in their tracks and looked quizzically at the yellow blob.

"What's…" began Bazza, but he never got to finish his question.

The yellow snot hit him square on the forehead. It sent him reeling backwards. He staggered about, using his arms for balance like a tightrope walker on the high wire. He held his forehead and tried to speak, but he couldn't find any words. Bang! Before he could recover, the snot hit him again. This time it walloped his bulging belly. He doubled over and sagged to his knees, gasping for air.

At this point his minions had seen enough and, like the rats they were, deserted the sinking ship. But for good measure, I sent out the snot in two rapid-fire blasts, smacking their bouncing bum cheeks as they scarpered. They yelped and shrieked, clutching their snot-stung buttocks as they made a hasty retreat.

I walked over to Bazza. He was badly winded and still hunched over on the floor. He cowered away from me, fearing another attack.

"Please don't hurt me. Please don't. I'll never touch you or your mate again," he wailed.

"I'll hold you to that. Now get out of here, and don't you dare mention this to anyone. Pass that on to your mates too," I instructed.

Bazza clambered to his feet and staggered off, holding his head with one hand and his belly with the other.

Frank made his way over to me. "Thanks, Scott. You saved me from a beating."

"No problem," I replied, looking at the pulsing blob of snot sitting in the palm of my hand. "I don't think Bazza and his boys will pose us any more problems."

The afternoon passed quietly after the fun and

games of lunch. Before we knew it, Frank and I were making our way home.

"We need to celebrate today's victory," I said. "Fancy an ice cream?"

"Great idea," replied Frank as we turned into Ida's Ices.

The shop was always bustling with children eager to sample Ida's latest ice cream. She regularly invented new flavours and had recently added tangy tomato and fizzy peach to the wide selection of weird and wacky flavours on offer.

After joining the lengthy queue and waiting our turn, we were eventually served. "Lemon meringue flavour for me, please," I said.

"And rhubarb for me," added Frank.

We watched as Ida scooped out the soft ice cream and placed the colourful dollops into two cones. We handed over our cash and headed out into the street, licking the ice cream before it melted in the afternoon heat.

As we walked along, I picked up on a commotion coming from across the street. High-pitched screams and wails filled the air. There was a large building site where a new supermarket was under construction. A huge stone pillar at the top of the partially built structure leaned precariously over the street. Men in yellow jackets and hard hats were scattering in all directions, desperately waving their arms and shouting at the top of their voices. The stone pillar was tilted at a worrying angle and it looked ready to topple at any second.

"Here, hold my ice cream," I said to Frank, handing him my cone. I delved into my pocket and pulled out the snot ball. It still pulsed and throbbed, but was now covered in bits of fluff and pocket debris.

The snot ball had proved useful on smaller objects, but this lump of stone was much larger and I wasn't convinced it'd be effective. Then I had an ingenious idea. I sneaked a finger up my right nostril and began to claw down more mucus. Long yellow strings appeared, which I added to the existing ball. I was like a magician pulling handkerchiefs from a hat. More and more snot just kept coming. Switching nostrils, I started to unpack the contents from the other side. Frank watched in disbelief, his mouth gaping open as melted ice cream dripped from the cones.

In no time at all, I'd transformed the golf ball-sized projectile into the size of a cricket ball. I looked up, the chunk of stone was still dangerously close to toppling. Rubble cascaded down to the street below. If the pillar fell, it would cause catastrophic damage as there were still people milling around despite the best attempts of the builders to move them away. It'd be a miracle if lives weren't lost.

The snot ball was heavy now and too big to flick. I'd no option but to launch it overarm. I focused all of my attention on the stone block which was now at the point of tumbling. With all my might, I launched the mucus projectile. It flew like a rocket before walloping the huge stone pillar and knocking it back. But the stone was still not secure and it remained dangerously close to falling.

As soon as the snot ball was back in my hand, I fired it again. It thudded into the block. This time the stone column tilted even further back, closer to its original position. My gut feeling told me that one more good whack should do it.

To get maximum power, I took a run up and used every ounce of force I could muster. It felt like my shoulder was going to pop out of the socket. Whack! The stone pillar tipped back into place. I'd done it!

People on the street had gathered to watch the drama unfold and they began to jubilantly clap and cheer. Some of the onlookers approached me to offer their congratulations and pat me on the back. I felt like a real-life superhero. My quick thinking had saved the day and I was bursting with pride.

* * *

Unfortunately, the secret about my super snot was out. After lots of tests and medical check-ups, it was decided that I'd be allowed to continue my allergy treatment. That was a huge relief.

My super-charged snot gained a serious amount of public attention and the government showed a particular interest. Government scientists are currently testing my mutated mucus in the hope of creating a new state-of-the-art piece of non-fatal weaponry. It'll be called 'Scott Stott's Hot-Shot Snot'. I'll also be paid handsomely. The six-figure pay cheque I've been promised is definitely not something to be sniffed at!

A Pat On The Head

Mum gazed into the full-length mirror as she brushed her fiery red hair. The reflection which stared back captured her beauty perfectly and only confirmed to me that Mum was the prettiest lady in the whole world.

While lying on Mum's bed and watching her get ready, I'd also been examining the contents of her jewellery box. I'd been pretending I was a royal princess preparing for a ball, carefully slipping on one of the many rings which she stored in the box.

Mum turned and saw what I was doing. Her lovely smile was replaced by a miserable frown. Puzzled by her sudden change in expression, and fearing that I was in the wrong, I quickly pulled the ring from my finger and placed it back in the jewellery box.

"I'm sorry, Amy," Mum said in a quiet voice.

"I didn't mean to scowl. Most of those rings were Gran's prized possessions. The way things are looking we may have to sell them to keep our heads above water."

I sat up on the bed and gazed at the jewellery before staring back at Mum. "Surely things aren't that bad? We don't need money so desperately, do we?" I asked, fearing that the answer wouldn't be the one I wanted to hear.

Mum put her brush on the dressing table and walked over to sit next to me. Her eyes were glassy with tears, so I reached out, taking her hand and forcing a hopeful smile.

"Money's really tight at the minute, Amy. Since your dad left, I've been doing my best to make ends meet. If I'm honest though, we're struggling," she explained, as tears trickled down her cheeks, smudging her freshly applied make-up before plopping off her chin.

I turned and put my arms around Mum. She hugged me back and I held her tightly, letting her fragrant perfume waft up my nostrils. "I'll do anything at all, you know I will. We'll get through this one way or another," I reassured her.

"Oh Amy, you're amazing!" Mum said between gulps and sniffles as tears continued to stream down her cheeks. She pulled the jewellery box across the bed cover and sifted through the contents. "Most of these rings aren't worth a lot, but they hold a lot of sentimental value. There's one ring which Gran always said was worth a fair bit." Mum picked up a simple gold ring and inspected it carefully. "I think this is the one but it looks just like the others. Gran loved to buy lots of similar-looking rings. Your gran knew what she liked and she liked what she knew."

I took the ring from Mum and studied it carefully. A flood of happy memories cascaded into my mind. I remembered the times Gran read me bedtime stories before tenderly kissing my forehead as I drifted off to sleep. I smiled at the thought of the happy times I'd spent with her helping out on the farm, mucking out the cattle and milking the cows.

"Can I trust you to do something for me?" Mum asked.

"Of course. You know I'll do anything to help," I replied.

"Please take this ring to Jott's Jewellers when they reopen tomorrow morning. Ask them to value it. If it's worth more than £2,000 get a cheque made out in my name. That should cover the bills for a couple of months until I come up with another plan," said Mum.

Reluctantly, I agreed. It was a heartbreaking decision to make, but it seemed our only option. I slipped the ring into my pocket and decided to grab some fresh air to clear my head, so I made my way out into the early morning sunshine.

Heading down the dirt track which ran from the farmhouse to the main road, my thoughts turned to Gran. She'd been the best and it upset me to think that we might have to sell one of the few remaining links we still had to her. Taking the ring from my pocket, I examined it as I walked.

I was completely in my own world and didn't spot a rock in the middle of the track. I caught it with my left foot and stumbled and staggered before I toppled over and landed in a cloud of dust. As I brushed myself down, a sudden wave of fear swept over me. The ring! Where was it?

I crawled on my hands and knees, frantically searching for Gran's ring in the stones and dust which covered the track. No joy! As I stood up, I glanced into the cow field on my left and to my utter relief I spotted the ring sitting on a tuft of grass near the fence. My relief turned to despair as I saw Edna the cow lumbering towards the grassy tuft.

"Edna! No, Edna!" I yelled, as the beast plodded closer and closer.

I sprinted towards the field, but the electrified fence stood in my way. I couldn't get over it without being zapped and the wires were too close together to climb between.

Edna was now standing next to the juicy tuft,

gormlessly gawping down at her next meal. She lowered her head and opened her jaws! I watched in horror as she ripped up the clump of grass, ring and all, and began to chew and munch. Her huge jaws moved sideways as she chomped and gobbled before she took one large gulp and the mouthful of food was swallowed. Gone!

I looked down at the patch of grass where the ring had been and my heart plummeted to my boots. It was now chewed down to the roots and there was no sign of Gran's ring. I felt a mixture of panic and confusion. Mum had entrusted me with the ring and now it was making its way through Edna's insides!

As I stared out across the field, an idea popped into my head. Edna's enclosure was a minefield of cow pats. There were fresh ones with flies buzzing around them and older, crusted ones which had baked hard like concrete in the hot sun. One thing was for sure, what goes in must come out and when that ring made its next appearance, I'd be able to get it back and Mum would be none the wiser. Or at least that was what I hoped.

Popping back to the farmhouse, I collected a piece of paper and a pencil. I then returned to the field and sketched out a map of the enclosure, carefully marking on the positions of the existing cow pats. I figured I didn't need to worry about the older, crusty ones as I was only interested in the fresh deposits. After double-checking that I'd recorded the existing pats correctly, I folded up the paper and headed back to the farmhouse. All I had to do now was wait for nature to take its course, and with a bit of luck, I'd find the ring before too long.

* * *

I made sure I was up before Mum the next day. Overnight, I'd considered which supplies I would need for my task and was hopeful I could lay my hands on them without needing to waste time going to the shop.

I grabbed a plastic bag from the stash we kept under the sink, then added a pair of rubber gloves. They were pink, but now wasn't the time to worry about such minor issues. There was no way on earth I was plunging my bare hands into cow muck! Spotting a pack of antibacterial wipes, I added them to the bag. I filled a bottle with water and placed that in too. I was guessing that the ring was going to need a good wash after its intestinal adventure. Finally, I dropped in a roll of kitchen towel. It would undoubtedly come in useful at some point as I feared a messy job lay ahead. Quietly leaving the house, I went to the shed for the last piece of equipment.

After rummaging through Dad's old gear, I found his swimming mask. The rubber had perished, but it would do the job. Eyewear was essential as cow poo in my peepers could cause me serious medical problems! It just didn't bear thinking about. I stuffed the mask into the bag. After checking that I still had the map in my pocket, I headed down to Edna's field. It was time to get Gran's ring back.

I entered the paddock, making sure the gate was closed behind me. The last thing I needed to deal with was an escaped cow. Pulling out the map, I decided it was best to mark on any pats which had recently appeared. As I made my way around the field, I was thrilled to find three new deposits which were nice and fresh. Black clouds of flies buzzed about, temporarily landing on the slimy mounds of poo before quickly flying off again.

I thought it best to start with the biggest pile first and pulled on the swimming mask, adjusting the strap until it fitted comfortably. The pink gloves were next. They went halfway up my forearms, which reduced the chances of any skin contamination. After giving my fingers a wiggle, I figured I was good to go.

After gulping as much fresh air as my lungs could hold, I dropped to my knees and plunged my hands into the steaming cow pat. The mound clearly hadn't been there long as it was still warm. The heat seeped through the rubber gloves and warmed my hands. Flies zigzagged around my head. I did my best to ignore them and to focus on the job in hand. Scooping up handfuls of Edna's freshly deposited dung, I sifted through her recent bowel movements. The brown slime oozed between my fingers as I searched and scoured. No sign of Gran's ring. I stood up, exhaled and then filled my lungs with fresh air before kneeling back down and looking again. After searching through the whole pile of poo, I conceded temporary defeat. One pat down, two to go.

I made my way to the next pile, preparing to repeat the procedure. It was at that moment I heard Mum calling me from the farmhouse. I couldn't let her see what I was up to! I hurried across the field and hid behind the feeding trough at the far end of the paddock.

Peeking under the metal trough, I could see Mum making her way down the track. She was calling my name but there was no way I could let her find me or else my plan would be rumbled. Out of the corner of my eye, I spotted Edna lolloping towards me. She thought it was feeding time.

"Shoo! Get away, you stupid creature. Shoo!" I hissed, fearing that the troublesome beast would give me away.

Edna continued until she was finally standing next to me. Then a long pink tongue slithered out of her mouth and licked the side of my face. It was like wet sandpaper being rubbed across my skin and it took everything I had not to throw up as her hot, sticky breath made me gag.

"You filthy beast! Get away!" I hissed. Crawling across the grass, but still remaining out of sight, I checked where Mum was. I could see her making her way back up the track. Shortly after, I heard the truck's engine fire up and watched as she drove off down the track before turning onto the main road. I gave it a minute or two until I was sure the coast was clear, then headed for cow pat number two to continue the search.

The next mound had a smaller circumference than the first. This one wasn't quite as fresh and the surface had begun to harden. I broke through the wafer-thin crust and delved deep into the brown slop beneath. Scooping out handful after handful, I felt carefully, checking every lump and praying that my fingers would fall upon the ring. I wafted away a swarm of flies which had descended like a cloud. Their buzzing was incessant and it rang in my ears and bounced around inside my head. I couldn't stand any more so I swatted at them. As I did, I caught the plastic cover of the mask, smearing poo across it and making it virtually impossible to see through.

I ripped off a couple of sheets of kitchen towel and tried to clean the mask, but I only succeeded in smearing the brown marks. I decided I'd just have to work around it.

I plunged my fingers deeper until I'd sifted through the lot, barely able to see what I was doing and relying heavily on my sense of touch. After the pat had been thoroughly checked, I stood up. I gulped in fresh air as the odds of discovering the ring drastically tumbled. There was one more pile of dung to go and I prayed that it would contain Gran's ring.

I blindly staggered over to the third and final cow pat, peered up to the sky and silently asked Gran for some assistance. If she was looking down on me, now would be a perfect time to help out. I dropped to my knees, pulled apart the sloppy poo and sifted through the lukewarm remains of Edna's last meals. Suddenly my fingers felt a hard object. My heart skipped a beat. I pulled the mystery find out of the sludge, held it up and did my best to look at it through the poo-smeared mask.

Coated in bits of half-digested food waste, was the ring. I smiled broadly and placed it on the grass. With Edna lurking close by, I covered it with my trainer to avoid a repeat of yesterday's incident. Pulling off one of the gloves, and taking great care to avoid contaminating my skin, I removed the bottle from the bag and poured the water over the ring. I wiped the recovered piece of jewellery with a piece of kitchen towel and smiled to myself. Unfortunately, it was at that moment my plan began to fall apart.

Mum was driving up the track and before I could react, she spotted me and began to beep the horn repeatedly. After pulling over and parking the truck, she opened the gate and began to make her way across the field.

"I need to explain," I said, still wearing a single poo-coated pink glove and Dad's dung-smeared mask.

"No, me first," said Mum, giving me a quizzical look. "I looked all over for you, but I couldn't find you anywhere. I wanted to let you know that I'd given you the wrong ring. It had no financial value. I'm so sorry, but I did tell you they all looked similar. I've just been to town and reluctantly sold Gran's real ring. We can cover the bills for a while now as I got a good price."

I stared at the ring in my hand and tried to take in what Mum was telling me. I'd been on my hands and knees all morning, sifting through cow pat after cow pat and all along I was searching for a ring which was essentially worth zilch. I dropped to my knees and shook my head.

Mum pointed at something over my shoulder. Her mouth was hanging open and her words seemed to be stuck in her throat. Turning around, I was met by a horrifying sight.

Edna's bottom was inches away from my face and

her tail was raised. Before I could move, it happened. It was a moment which will haunt me for the rest of my life. Edna let rip a foul torrent. A cascading deluge of steaming cow poo! I tried to move but I couldn't compete with the rate at which she was evacuating her innards. The vile sludge splattered onto my head and slithered and glooped down my face. I pinched my nose and tightly closed my mouth. Within a few seconds, the putrid brown waterfall had ended and the warm deposit flowed down my T-shirt and jeans before dribbling onto the grass. She lowered her tail and swished it from side to side before mooching off across the field, unaware of the vile situation she'd caused. I was left on my hands and knees, caked from head to toe in a brown suit of steaming cow poo.

Slowly regaining my feet, I waddled back to the farmhouse where Mum hosed me down in the yard.

From that day on, I was always honest with Mum when I knew I was in the wrong. I've definitely learnt my lesson and have never tried to pull the wool over her eyes since. My reward from Mum is a pat on the head, which I must say is a lot more pleasant than the one which I received from Edna.

Fish Out Of Water

I used to hate swimming lessons. I felt sick when we were queuing for the bus to the local baths. I hid my trunks under my bed or 'forgot' my towel so that I could sit and watch rather than enduring forty minutes of water torture. If I did make it into the pool, I wailed so much that I couldn't breathe. The instructor had to pull me out with a pole, even though I was in the learner pool. Taking all of that into account, you probably wouldn't believe me if I told you that I'm a record-breaking swimmer. I can see the puzzled expression on your face. How did I go from the kid who was terrified of water into a swimming superstar? I'll explain what happened, right from the beginning.

* * *

Although I hated swimming, I used to spend hours near water for a completely different reason. Fishing was my passion. I'd spend all of my spare time sitting on the riverbank, watching the world go by and waiting for a fish to nibble on my bait. I wasn't very good at it though. Most of the time, I caught absolutely nothing. Sometimes I caught a cold as I was out in all weathers. But on one memorable occasion, I actually caught a fish.

I'll never forget the float bobbing, prompting me to grab my rod. After a few seconds the orange-tipped float gently slid under the water. I raised the rod and began to reel in my catch. The end of the rod bent over and I could feel a pulling sensation. There was definitely something on the hook! As I wound in the reel and lifted the rod, my eyes were fixed on the line which zipped around as the fish darted in different directions. Before long the fish appeared on the surface. After months of frustration, I'd finally caught something.

I slipped my net under the fish, lifted it out and placed it on the bank, eager to have a closer look. Dropping to my knees, I gently searched inside the net and there it was. Not the biggest fish ever and definitely not a record catch, but it meant the world to me. I was thrilled to bits. Slipping the hook from its mouth, I picked the fish up and carefully held it. The sun reflected on its silver scales and I noticed multicoloured stripes running from head to tail. It had large, bulbous eyes and a strangely shaped dorsal fin with a series of spines running across its edge. I'd seen loads of pictures of species of fish, but this creature was completely different. It was unlike anything I'd seen in my fishing books and magazines.

Not wanting to harm the creature or stress it out, I walked through the long grass to the river to slip it back into the water. As I bent down and reached out to release it, the fish began to wriggle. Suddenly, I felt a searing pain in the palm of my hand, like red-hot needles being stabbed into my flesh. The pain was excruciating, but fortunately short-lived. The fish twisted and flipped before sliding out of my hand and plopping back into the water. I watched as it scooted away back into the depths.

Inspecting my hand, I could see four pinprick blood spots on my palm. The fish had stabbed me with the spines on its fin! I took a tissue from my pocket and wiped my hand.

It was safe to say I'd used up all my fishing luck for the day, so I decided to head home. It had taken me this long to catch one fish, so the chances of following it up with another straight away looked unlikely. I packed up, slung my bag over my shoulder and made my way home.

After telling Mum and Dad all about my maiden catch, I headed to bed, feeling the full effects of a day spent in the fresh air. I was asleep as soon as my head hit the pillow. Unfortunately, my dreams that night caused me to sleep fitfully. I dreamed that I was swimming with a shoal of fish; darting and flitting through the weeds. I rose to the surface to gobble up flies as they drowned.

When my alarm woke me up the next morning, I felt more exhausted than the previous night. I considered my dreamy aquatic adventures. I'd never experienced anything like them. They felt so real. Putting the dreams down to the excitement of my first catch, I got dressed before going down for breakfast. I then headed off to school.

Everything was going smoothly until late morning. Mr Lake's history lesson was as dull as ditchwater and I battled to stay awake as he droned on and on. He was explaining about some battle which had taken place years ago where a bloke was shot in the eye with an arrow. I'm sure the actual event was really exciting, but unfortunately Mr Lake had a knack of making even the most incredible historical events sound so boring.

Without warning, my mouth began to feel dry and I had a sudden urge to get a drink. I raised my hand to get Mr Lake's attention. He eventually broke off from his historical ramblings to give me permission to leave. I headed out to the drinking fountain on the corridor and gulped and glugged the refreshing water. After several mouthfuls, my thirst was quenched, but my skin had started to feel dry and itchy. It was a strange sensation and one which I'd never experienced before. I allowed the fountain to spray on my face. It cooled me and soothed my skin. Feeling re-energised, I headed back to class.

The strange feeling didn't return until later in the day when I was heading home. As I walked through the town centre with the sun beating down, my skin felt as dry as the Sahara Desert. I felt like a sponge that had been squeezed out so tightly every last droplet was removed.

I spotted the ornamental fountain which had been in the town square for as long as I could remember. The water gushed from the mouth of a stone dolphin and showered down into the pool below, where cans and other debris floated about.

Out of nowhere, I was gripped by an overwhelming urge to climb into the water. This just wasn't me. I was the kid who hated water, but I suddenly had a burning desire to dive into the public fountain.

An urge to take off my clothes swept over me. I peeled off my shirt and tie before kicking off my shoes. I tried to resist, but it was no use. I unzipped my trousers and stepped out of them. Finally, I kicked off my undies. I was as naked as the day I'd been born!

People gasped and gawked. A concerned woman covered a young child's eyes with her hands, not wanting the innocent kid to witness my disgraceful display of public nudity. Some older kids were snapping pictures and recording video footage of me with their phones, causing me to cover my nakedness with my hands.

Looking back, it was a weird experience. I felt like a puppet being controlled by someone else. I was drawn to the water like a steel can being pulled towards a magnet. I moved across the square at lightning speed. To halt myself, I grabbed hold of a lamp post and held on tight. It was no use. My legs just wanted to carry me to the fountain and my grip on the post was broken. Before I knew it, I was clambering into the chilly water.

An even bigger crowd had now gathered. Shoppers pointed and laughed. I was making a real spectacle of myself. I guess they thought I was some stupid kid taking part in a dare, or that I was the school joker who'd decided to take one prank a little bit too far. But they were wrong. My actions were completely out of my control.

I submerged myself in the water and it soothed my skin. I had the urge to kick my legs and even though the water was only shallow, I propelled myself along. I was the boy who not long ago would have wailed like a baby at the prospect of having to put his face in the water at the swimming pool. Now I was swimming breaststroke among the floating crisp packets and cigarette butts in the public fountain.

My aquatic experience turned out to be short-lived. A heavy hand grabbed hold of me and hauled me over the edge of the fountain before dumping me on the pavement. Looking up and shielding my eyes from the sun, I could make out the figure of PC Pond, the local police officer.

"Do you realise it's a criminal offence to strip naked and bathe in the public fountain?" asked PC Pond, covering up my modesty with his police helmet.

"I'm sorry. I honestly don't know what came over me," I said, scraping back my hair.

"Put on some clothes then I'll take you home. I think I need a chat with your parents," he said, gesturing towards my school uniform which was scattered across the town square.

Needless to say, Mum and Dad went absolutely ballistic! I'd never seen my folks so close to physically imploding due to their atomic levels of rage!

"What do you think you're playing at, Corey? First we can't get you near a swimming pool and now you're doing backstroke naked in the fountain!" bellowed Dad, after PC Pond had left.

"It was breaststroke," I said meekly.

"I don't care what it was!" roared Dad. "You've humiliated us. Our family will be a laughing stock!"

"I'm absolutely horrified," sobbed Mum as she dabbed at her eyes with a crumpled tissue. "You've brought shame on this family."

I decided the less said the better, so I remained silent. My bizarre behaviour was so unbelievable that I didn't blame them for their response.

"Get upstairs and have a warm shower before you catch pneumonia. You're dripping and you'll ruin the laminate flooring," moaned Dad, calming down a little.

"And you're grounded until further notice," added Mum.

Squelching upstairs, leaving wet footprints in my wake, I stripped off before getting into the shower.

I stood under the warm water and allowed it to flow over my skin. It felt incredible and before I knew it, the skin on my fingers and toes began to wrinkle. I reached out to turn the water off, but my hand kept missing the controls. It was like someone trying to push the north poles of two magnets together. Every time I attempted to switch off the water, an invisible force diverted my hand. I tried to step out of the shower, but my feet were fastened to the shower tray. I was trapped! Would I turn into a human prune if I stayed in the shower forever? Would my body shrivel up into a withered sack of skin? I panicked and threw myself out of the shower, landing on the bathroom floor with an almighty thud.

I heard heavy footsteps on the stairs and before I could cover my nakedness, the door opened and Mum received a full view of me in all my glory!

"What's happened? Are you alright?" asked Mum in a concerned tone.

"Er…I slipped and fell," I lied, getting to my knees and covering myself with a towel. "I'll be fine, honestly."

Mum looked at me and shook her head before closing the door.

Sitting on my bed, I quietly contemplated the bizarre sequence of events from that day. How had I suddenly changed from a kid who hated water to one who seemed to be magnetised towards the stuff? Rubbing the palm of my hand, I looked at the four tiny marks which the fish had inflicted. A crazy idea dawned on me. Surely that fish couldn't be behind my watery mishaps. Or could it?

* * *

The next morning, I was up for school at the crack of dawn. I went out of my way to avoid Mum and Dad and also steered clear of any water sources.

Crossing the school yard, I headed to the sports hall

for PE. I was first to arrive, but by the time I'd got changed some of the other boys had begun to drift in.

"Have you dried off yet after your little dip?" mocked Tim Trickler, who was widely recognised as the school joker. "Gutted I missed your little swimming session, I'd have loved to get it on film to share it online."

The other boys chuckled, but I remained silent. There was nothing I could say. Anything I did come up with would just make the situation worse.

"Right, lads," said Mr Drench, as he burst into the changing room, "I'm after a massive favour. I need someone to swim in the Hawley Swimming Gala this afternoon. Don't worry about kit, I'll sort you out. Come on, fellas, I'm desperate."

The teacher's request was met by a deafening wall of silence until Tim Trickler piped up again.

"What about Corey Spring? He's good at making a big splash," he said, unwilling to drop yesterday's fountain fiasco.

"This isn't a joke, lad!" snapped Mr Drench. "I'll have you know that my job's on the line. I'm under pressure from the Head. If I can't enter a full team, we're disqualified. And if we get disqualified, he's threatened to sack me. I've got a holiday in Barbados and a sports car to pay for. How can I do that if I'm out of a job?"

Mr Drench cradled his head in his hands as the changing room fell silent again. You could have heard a pin drop.

"I'll do it," I said, feeling no fear at the prospect of having to get in the swimming pool which had proved to be my arch-nemesis for so long. "I've had some private lessons. I'm much more confident now," I lied.

The other boys sniggered and laughed but Mr Drench looked at me without uttering a word, desperation written all over his face. He turned and headed into his office before returning with a pair of trunks and a towel which he hurled in my direction. "You're in, lad," he said. "I appreciate this so much. You're a lifesaver!"

"You'll need someone to save his life and drag him out when he's drowning," giggled Tim Trickler, sparking the other boys into raucous laughter.

Mr Drench roared at them, but I took no notice of their jibes. I rubbed the palm on my left hand and stared at the indentations which were just about visible. I felt no fear at all. Previously, the thought of swimming would have made my blood run cold, but not now. As crazy as it may sound, I was convinced the strange fish had done something to me and I was about to put my theory to the test.

* * *

Standing on the side of the pool with my toes hanging over the edge was easy. Usually my knees would have been knocking and I'd have been gripped by fear, but as I waited for the starting gun I felt like I was born to swim. The dry feeling had returned to my skin and I fought the overwhelming urge to get into the water. My heart thumped in my chest and I felt strong and powerful.

"On your marks, get set…" called the official before firing his starting pistol.

I dived elegantly into the pool and entered the water with barely a splash. I used my feet to power myself along. Glancing both ways, I could see that I was already ahead by a distance. Breaking the surface of the water, I heard a deafening roar as the noise echoed around the building, creating an incredible atmosphere. I fed off the buzz of the crowd. I kicked my feet and pulled with my hands, generating a tremendous amount of power. It all felt so easy. It was effortless. I was barely trying but I was miles ahead of the others who were straining every sinew to even keep close to me.

Ducking under the water and pushing off the wall, I began my second length. The other boys were barely halfway through their first. I flashed them a confident smile as I powered past, sending a frothy wake surging across the pool.

I could see Mr Drench leaping up and down like his feet were on fire. His eyes were wide with delight and disbelief. The kid he regularly struggled to get on the swimming bus, let alone in the water, was leading the race by a mile. I was delivering an aquatic masterclass!

As I reached out for the side, I knew I'd easily won. The crowd were on their feet. They were going wild. I waved and punched the air as I bobbed up and down.

Climbing out and sitting on the poolside, I tried to take in my achievement. Mr Drench bounded over like an excited dog.

"You've just broken the junior world swimming record. I can't believe what I've seen. You were like a fish!" babbled Mr Drench. "You've saved my job too. After twenty years of PE teaching, I finally have a winning child to my name. I can't thank you enough, Corey," he said, vigorously patting me on the shoulder as he excitedly hopped from foot to foot.

I'll never forget my moment on the winning podium when the medal was placed around my neck. The crowd raucously applauded and cheered. That's a memory I'll definitely treasure for the rest of my life.

* * *

So there you have it. I decided it was for the best to keep things quiet about the mysterious fish which had clearly passed on some sort of super swimming ability. The last thing I wanted was to be poked and prodded by doctors and scientists.

I've now got my sights set on the Olympics in four years' time. With some extra practice, just think how fast I'll be by then. Gold medal, here I come!

The Root Of The Problem

Everything started to go wrong when Gran left me to do a spot of gardening while she popped to the shops. It turned out the events that day would leave me traumatised for the rest of my life!

* * *

I opened the shed door and a musty smell hit me. The confined space was packed with spades, brushes and all types of gardening equipment. I stepped in, making sure the mower lead, which was strewn across the floor, didn't trip me. Carefully navigating my way through the minefield of potential hazards, I made it to the back of the shed. The seed shelf was high up on the wall and I had to stand on my tiptoes to get to it. Earlier, Gran had instructed me to plant some seeds but I was paying little attention at the time, so I'd completely forgotten which ones she'd mentioned.

There were loads of different seeds; some were in packets, one batch was in a small glass jar and others were in open, shallow trays. They all looked the same and if I'm honest I was left feeling pretty clueless.

At one end of the shelf, I spotted a small container, roughly the size of a matchbox. The lid was bound with tape and a red cross had been drawn on the side. I shook the container and something inside rattled. I was intrigued, so I lifted it down and peeled off the tape.

When I opened the lid and tipped out the contents, I was surprised at what I found. The seeds were triangular. They were unlike anything I'd ever seen and were much larger than the others on the shelf. I vaguely remembered Gran telling me that the seeds were quite large, so presumed these were the ones. I put them back in the container and replaced the lid. On my way out, I picked up a small shovel and headed to the garden.

The soil was soft after the previous night's rain, so the digging was easy. Gran had left written instructions to dig down about ten centimetres and evenly space out the holes. I unscrewed the lid and popped in some seeds. As I'd no more room, I left the remaining seeds in the container and shoved it in the pocket of my shorts. Finally, I covered the seeds with soil and watered them before returning the shovel. I then headed indoors as I desperately needed the toilet.

Dropping my shorts and undies and sitting down, I felt the cold toilet seat chill my bare bottom. I'd a feeling I was going to be there a while, so I leaned over to get a magazine from the shelf. As I leafed through the pages, I went through the motions, quite literally. Just as I'd finished and was about to flush, I started to feel vibrations in my bottom. The toilet seat felt like it was shaking. Now, I realise that my toilet habits are sometimes a little extreme, especially if I've had one of Gran's super-spicy curries for instance, but this was ridiculous.

I stood up, shorts and undies still round my ankles, and flushed the toilet. The contents of the toilet bowl, rather than flushing, began to rise up. For a moment, I started to fear a flood, but suddenly it plummeted down and disappeared round the U-bend. But the toilet didn't refill. Instead, it began to wobble and shake more violently. I pulled my pants up and stepped back. At that moment something emerged from the toilet!

I say 'something', because at the time I'd no idea what it was. Plus, I was used to seeing things disappear down the loo rather than appear from it. I mean, how many times has a plant root ever popped up from your toilet?

Yep, you heard me right, a root! A brown, hairy, slithering root! It snaked its way over the edge of the toilet seat and reached out towards me like an outstretched finger. I was fixed to the spot with shock. My mind whirred and I tried to figure out what was happening. Mrs Anderson, my teacher, had taught us that plants grow slowly. She definitely never mentioned them appearing from a toilet, that's for sure!

The root was moving at an incredible speed and by now it was steadily creeping across the tiled floor.

I opened the door and made my exit, stumbling into the hallway and landing on my backside. The snake-like root was still coming for me. It was slithering across the mat, making its way towards the open door. I reached out my leg and kicked the door shut. The catch engaged. I knelt up and crawled over, putting my ear to the wood and listening intently. I couldn't hear anything. Maybe the strain involved in going to the toilet had caused me to have some sort of bizarre hallucination. Was that even possible?

Suddenly the door began to gently shake and rattle. In the gap between door and carpet, the root appeared! It crept towards me and I backed away in horror. Getting to my feet, I made for the kitchen, but I was stopped in my tracks.

Emerging from the sink was a second root which must have entered the house through the drain. It was thicker than the toilet root and was waving around in the air like a snake being charmed from a basket. The root turned towards me before growing down and scrabbling across the kitchen floor.

I swivelled my head and saw the first root heading in my direction! Turning on my heels, I sprinted back the way I'd come and launched myself over the first invader. As I was airborne, I looked down and I swear the root reached up to grab my trailing foot! Fortunately, it didn't succeed. I hit the ground running and dashed for the front door.

I pushed down on the handle but it wouldn't budge. Gran must have locked it on her way out. I turned to see both roots coming down the hallway towards me. They twisted and twirled. They wriggled and jiggled. I decided it was far too risky to jump them both to get to the back door so my only option was to head upstairs. Roots couldn't climb stairs. Or at least that's what I was hoping.

I vaulted the carpeted stairs two at a time. As I landed on the top step, I turned and looked back. There was no sign of the rampaging roots. My thoughts raced as I tried to make sense of what was happening.

My relief was short-lived as I spotted the roots appearing around the end of the banister, creeping towards me. They swiftly scaled the stairs and within a few seconds had made it up the first five. I'd no option. I had to move. I headed for my bedroom up in the attic, but as I was crossing the landing a horrifying sight met my eyes. A third root was now emerging from the upstairs bathroom and was moving with menace towards me.

I pulled down the ladder which I used to get to my room. It clicked and clunked before locking into position. I clambered up the metal rungs, but stopped mid-way to look back. All three roots had now converged on the ladder and were entwining themselves around the metal rungs. I continued my ascent and pulled myself up through the opening. Leaning back through the gap, I tried to raise the ladder, but the roots were so entangled it wouldn't budge. The terrible trio were snaking their way closer to the attic opening.

My mind raced and my heart pounded against my ribcage. How was this going to end? Was I going to be killed by these ruthless roots? A chill coursed through my body. I grabbed the attic hatch and slammed it shut. Because of the ladder, I couldn't lock it so I decided to sit on the hatch. I waited. I listened. Nothing. Then I picked out what sounded like a scuffling, scratching noise coming from underneath me. The hatch began to lift!

I could feel it begin to rise despite my full body weight being slumped on it. I reached out and grabbed a shoe just as one of the roots appeared from the gap between the hatch and the floor. Gripping the shoe, I repeatedly bashed the root and it began to recoil. Before I knew it the other two had forced their way through. I smashed them over and over with the shoe. It was just like those games on the funfair where you've to hit pop-up targets with a big mallet. As fast as I walloped one, another reappeared.

Making a swift decision, I rolled off the hatch and the creeping roots seized their opportunity. They scrabbled across the floor towards me. I looked around for an escape route, but it seemed they had me cornered.

Above me was a long rectangular window. If I could climb through it, I'd be on the roof and I could signal for help. I clambered on my bedside table and pushed open the window. The gap created was just big enough for me to squeeze through. I grabbed the metal edge and lifted myself up.

Suddenly I felt something grab my left trainer. One of the roots had latched on to my laces and I was caught in the middle of a tug of war. I frantically kicked with my free foot until the trainer slipped off. In one swift movement, I dragged myself up onto the tiled roof and slammed the window shut. The roots prodded and poked at the glass, still desperate to continue their unrelenting pursuit. Fortunately, there was no way they were going to get through the window.

I scanned the street below. It was deserted. Usually someone was about, but today there wasn't a soul in sight. The tiles were slick from the rain and I was terrified I'd slip off. The garden below looked a long way down and I didn't fancy my chances if I fell.

Sliding down the slippery tiles on my bottom, I edged further down the roof. Suddenly, the skylight window began to open. The roots were now slithering across the slates. I moved even further down, but I was running out of roof. It was at that moment that my lone trainer lost all grip and I began to slide. I desperately reached out and clawed at the tiles. My trainer squeaked and squealed on the wet slates as I tried to use it as a makeshift brake. It was no use. I hurtled over the edge of the roof.

Fortunately, I managed to cling on to the plastic guttering. It flexed and wobbled under my weight. I tried to kick my feet back up but the more I tried, the more the guttering creaked and groaned. I could see the screws pulling out of the wall. I didn't have long left before the whole lot would give way. To add to my problems, the roots had appeared over the edge of the roof and were reaching down towards me. It looked like it was game over. I'd either fall to my death or be killed by the rampant roots!

With a loud crack the guttering came away from the wall. Everything seemed to happen in slow motion.

I appeared to temporarily hang in the air for a split second before I started to plummet towards the ground.

Some people say that when you're about to die your life flashes before your eyes. Well mine did. Images and long-forgotten memories raced through my mind as I accepted my number was up.

Unexpectedly though, it turned out that my final moment hadn't arrived. Something quite incredible happened.

As I braced myself for the impact, my fall was suddenly halted. After a split-second pause, I hesitantly opened my eyes and found the world had been flipped upside down. I was dangling head first. I looked up to see the roots attached to my right ankle. They'd grabbed me and stopped me just in the nick of time. My mind raced as the roots began to gently lower me down until I was flat on my back on the concrete. My legs felt like jelly and I resisted the urge to stand for fear of puddling back down to the floor.

Just as I was calming down and taking in the crazy events of the last few minutes, the roots began to slowly move up my leg. The fine hairs tickled my skin. It was a weird sensation. The fear had gone now though. If the roots had saved my life, I was pretty sure they weren't going to harm me. They crept up to my shorts before disappearing into the pocket.

After a few seconds, the roots started to retract and they reappeared with the container of seeds. One of the roots was wrapped tightly around the container and the others navigated it along. Gently releasing their grip on my ankle, they headed back up towards the roof. They'd never meant me any harm, it seemed all they wanted was to retrieve their seedlings. My brain was scrambled!

When my legs felt strong enough to hold me, I got to my feet and went back into the house. The roots which had emerged from the kitchen sink were nowhere to be seen. I tentatively opened the toilet door, half expecting to see a root popping out from the loo, but apart from the water, the toilet bowl was empty. After checking upstairs, I decided the roots had what they wanted, so had returned to where they'd come from.

Just as I was about to slump on the sofa, I heard Gran's voice. She came into the lounge carrying two heavy-looking shopping bags.

"Are you okay? You look a bit pale," said Gran in a concerned tone.

I'd a feeling it was easier not to explain the root rampage to Gran. I doubted she'd believe me anyway.

"Yeah, I'm good," I replied. "What have you been buying?" I asked, trying to move the conversation on.

Gran put down the bags and reached into one of them.

"Thought we could do some gardening together," she said excitedly, holding up a packet of seeds.

Needless to say, I left Gran to it. The whole experience had taught me that gardening was definitely too dangerous for me!

Snapshock

Amanda stared into the mirror in the girls' toilets. She despised the reflection which peered back. Her eyes were drawn to the clusters of spots which littered her face like huge red volcanoes. Despite her best efforts to cover them up with make-up, they poked through the mask, determined to remain on show to the world.

Sighing deeply, Amanda picked up her school bag and slung it over her shoulder before heading out into the corridor. It amazed her how spiteful some of her peers could be and it was always a successful day if she managed to make it to the final bell with only a few cruel remarks. Life was harsh and one of the main reasons was Roxanne.

If looks were money, Roxanne would've been a millionaire. Her skin was flawless and her beauty left

Amanda feeling envious. The other girls fawned over her and paid her endless compliments which she lapped up, causing her already huge ego to swell even further. Unfortunately, Roxanne's beautiful exterior wasn't matched on the inside. Internally she was more like a barbed-wire fence. Plenty of kids had received a lashing from her acidic tongue. She regularly took great delight in highlighting Amanda's facial flaws in particular, usually in front of her peers for maximum humiliation value.

"Here she is," called Roxanne as Amanda approached the main exit, head down and shoulders hunched. "Come on, Pizza Face, let's have a look at you," she instructed, placing a hand on Amanda's shoulder to halt her progress. Reaching out her other hand, she lifted Amanda's chin. The other girls cackled and sniggered, causing a red bloom to swell across the embarrassed girl's cheeks. A lone tear trickled down her face, slaloming its way through the maze of spots. "You've got your Halloween mask on. You'll be scaring the younger kids if you're not careful." The other girls fell about laughing as Amanda desperately tried to hold back more tears.

Sensing the opportunity to make a break for it, she turned on her heels and bolted down the corridor. She barged through the emergency doors and merged with the masses of children who were heading home. Tears fell freely down her cheeks now. She wiped at them with the sleeve of her school jumper, creating a smeared mess of smudged make-up.

Arriving home, Amanda burst through the front door. She threw her bag down and headed upstairs before flopping onto her bed. She buried her face in her pillow and sobbed. Why did she have to be the one cursed with chronic spots? Life just wasn't fair!

* * *

Desperate not to let on to her mum about the persistent bullying, Amanda washed her face and tried to calm down. As she walked out of the bathroom, she heard the front door open.

"Hey, love. I'm back. You okay?" shouted Mum.

"Yeah, not bad," Amanda lied, making her way downstairs.

Amanda's mum delved into her coat pocket and handed her daughter a small blue leaflet.

"I think you should enter," said Mum. "You need to get a move on though, the deadline is the end of the week."

Amanda sat down and scanned the paper. Emblazoned across the top in bold writing, it read 'Flockborough Young Talent Show' and it went on to explain the rules and entry details.

"You've got a beautiful singing voice and I'm sure

people would love to hear it," encouraged Mum.

The thought of standing on a stage with the entire village watching her spots pulsing uncontrollably made Amanda's stomach flip. People wouldn't be able to concentrate on her voice as they'd be staring at the red blotches littered across her face.

"I'm not sure," Amanda replied, just as Dad arrived home from work.

"Take a look at what I've got for you," Dad said excitedly. "Mum said you're entering the talent contest, so I've treated you to a new camera to capture it all. You can take some shellfishes or whatever they're called."

"Selfies," Amanda said, watching carefully as Dad placed a bag on the kitchen table. He then proceeded to remove a strange-looking object. It looked nothing like the modern cameras she'd seen in the shops. He handed it to Amanda and she inspected it closely.

"It's not quite a state-of-the-art thing, but it's the best I could afford. The bloke in the charity shop said it can do everything the expensive ones can. It's got a stack of special features, but no handbook, unfortunately. Sure you'll work it out though," said Dad.

"Get that form filled in and I'll hand it in tomorrow when I'm in town," said Mum.

Amanda felt the crushing weight of expectation

bearing down on her. Even though she knew the whole thing would be a horrible experience, she didn't have the heart to dash her parents' hopes and enthusiasm.

"Okay, I'll enter," Amanda reluctantly replied.

Mum and Dad hugged their daughter. Amanda hugged them back and forced a smile which barely disguised the fear and turmoil which she was feeling.

* * *

Amanda completed the form and gave it to her mum. She then decided to try out her new camera, opting to make Snapper, her pet dog, the first model. Calling him upstairs, she listened as he eagerly bounded up and into her room before flopping down on the rug.

"Right, Snapper. Look at me. Come on," instructed Amanda. The dog ignored her, preferring to settle down on the rug instead.

Amanda pushed a square button. A red light blinked on top of the camera, with Snapper's image appearing in the digital viewfinder on the back. She moved the camera back and forth and twiddled with a dial on the side which made the dog's image larger and in focus.

"Smile, Snapper," she said as she pushed a triangular button. A bright flash illuminated the room and the dog leapt to his feet in surprise and confusion.

The poor creature blinked and pawed at its face, highly unimpressed by the unexpected explosion of light.

Amanda looked at the image frozen on the screen. It wasn't a bad picture but it seemed a little blurry. She clicked on the screen and a series of icons appeared. It seemed that she could alter the photo before she saved it. She swiped her finger across the blurred part of the picture and giggled as the dog's image began to get longer. He'd suddenly become a super-stretched sausage dog!

Glancing over the camera and looking at Snapper, she immediately stopped laughing. What she saw horrified her! Snapper's body was now twice as long and his belly was dragging on the floor. The dog turned its head quizzically and peered at its newly stretched torso. Amanda was dumbstruck. She quickly placed her finger on the screen and shortened the dog's body. Looking back at Snapper, she watched as his body began to shorten before eventually returning to its original length. What on earth was happening?

Placing a finger on the screen, she dragged the dog's whiskers, one by one, and stretched them until they were twice their original length. True to form, Snapper was sitting on the rug with extra long whiskers which nearly hung down to the floor! She quickly reduced them on the screen and the confused pooch gave a surprised yelp as his whiskers began to shrink.

This was more than enough for poor old Snapper. He trotted out and headed back downstairs.

Amanda's mind whirred. The camera was incredible and she had a feeling she was going to have some fun and games with it. For now though, she would keep quiet. She turned it off, stuffed it into the plastic bag and placed it under her bed.

* * *

The next morning, she stashed the camera in her school bag. Rather than dragging herself into school, she found that she had a spring in her step.

Unfortunately the buzz was short-lived as she sat down and waited for her first lesson to begin. Roxanne and her gaggle of groupies were deep in conversation. Amanda eavesdropped while rummaging in her pencil case.

"I'm a dead cert to win that talent show," bragged Roxanne. "How can my beauty fail to wow the judges?"

Amanda's heart sank. It was going to be tough enough to get up on that stage and Roxanne would only make things harder. How was being beautiful a talent anyway? Then again, it wasn't an issue that she didn't actually have any talent. Roxanne's dad was on the judging panel. He'd probably rig it so that his little darling won.

"Oi, Spotty," called out Roxanne. "Are you entering the talent show?"

Amanda ignored the comment, instead pretending to read the textbook opened in front of her.

"Are those spots affecting your hearing?" taunted Roxanne. The group of hangers-on cackled.

Just as Roxanne was about to take the bait, the classroom door swung open. Mr Symon made his way into the room, staggering under the weight of a teetering pile of science equipment.

Roxanne's band of heckling hyenas scampered to their places. Amanda sighed with relief that she'd been saved from yet more humiliation.

After making a sharp exit at the end of the lesson, Amanda met up with her best mate, Garth. He was one of the few people in school who didn't stare at her spots or make comments.

They sat down on one of the wooden benches in the yard and Amanda waited for some younger kids to pass before pulling out the carrier bag. Garth watched inquisitively.

"I'm going to show you something amazing," Amanda said. Garth looked intrigued.

"Is it a camera?" he asked. "It looks ancient. Has your dad been visiting the charity shop again?"

Amanda turned on the camera and pointed it at Garth, making him smile and pose. Flash! Garth blinked and rubbed his eyes.

"Crikey! That's enough to blind me," he said.

Amanda was too busy to reply as she stared at the back of the camera and swiped her finger across the screen.

Suddenly Garth gasped and grabbed his face with both hands.

"Don't freak out," urged Amanda, placing a reassuring hand on Garth's knee. "I sort of know what I'm doing. You'll be fine. Trust me."

Amanda's words seemed to slightly reassure the boy. He slowly removed his hands from his face to reveal a nose which was at least three times the length it'd been only a short while earlier. Garth began to panic.

"W-what have you done? P-please make it normal again," he stammered.

Garth's nose began to shrink as Amanda manipulated the image on the viewfinder. The baffled lad grabbed at his rapidly reducing nostrils. Within seconds they'd returned to their original size.

"You've seriously fried my brain," said Garth. "You've got to explain what just happened. How did you do it?"

"I will. I'll tell you all about it on the way home. Meet me by the gates," replied Amanda as she turned off the camera and put it back in her bag. "Just promise you'll keep it a secret."

Still feeling his nose, he nodded and the pair went their separate ways.

* * *

On the way home, Amanda explained how she'd tweaked Garth's photo. She also filled him in on the incident involving Snapper.

Suddenly Amanda stopped in her tracks and grabbed hold of Garth's arm. "I've just had an idea! I reckon I know how I can shut up Roxanne once and for all," she said.

Beckoning Garth closer, Amanda whispered her cunning plan into his ear. When she'd finished, a broad grin broke out on his face.

"High-five me!" exclaimed Garth, slapping Amanda's hand. "That's genius. Oh I can't wait for the talent show. It's going to be a night to remember."

* * *

The evening of the show finally arrived. After hours of applying layer after layer of make-up, Amanda felt confident enough to take part.

She registered and joined the other children who were buzzing around backstage. The air was filled with a mixture of excitement and nervy anticipation.

She spotted a young boy juggling a collection of colourful balls and a girl in a glitzy outfit giving instructions to a small dog which was balancing on its hind legs. At the far end of the room, a girl dressed in a sparkly leotard was walking on her hands, weaving in and out of the other kids.

Suddenly Amanda felt a hand on her shoulder. She turned around.

"I can't believe you've actually bothered turning up," sneered Roxanne. "You're meant to entertain the audience tonight, not terrify them. It's a talent show, not a freak show." Out of nowhere, her group of bullying sidekicks appeared.

They made cruel jibes and slyly mocked Amanda, who could feel her confidence slowly draining away. She was handed a temporary reprieve when Mrs Green, the organiser and host, entered the room. The excited buzz died away to be replaced by an expectant silence.

"Right, kids, listen up. There's a running order which I'll post on the wall. Take note of your slot and make sure you're ready. We're on a tight schedule," said Mrs Green, as she stuck a large sheet of paper to the wall.

The kids swarmed around the poster to check their stage time. When Amanda finally got close enough to see, she noted that she was the final act. She'd follow Roxanne. That'd do nicely. It would allow her to execute a crucial part of her plan.

Sitting alone, Amanda battled her nerves. She watched the number of children dwindle as they were called to the side of the stage to await their big moment. She heard laughter and clapping from the audience. Eventually she was alone with Roxanne, who was confidently strutting around like she owned the place.

"Roxanne," called a voice, "it's your turn."

Amanda realised this was her golden opportunity.

"Roxanne, please can I get a picture?" asked Amanda, nervously clutching the camera.

At first, Roxanne was suspicious, warily eyeing Amanda and the camera. But when her ego overpowered her thinking, she saw it as just another opportunity to pose.

"It'll be nice for you to have a picture of real beauty," Roxanne said, fluffing her hair and pouting, which actually made her look a bit like a duck. "Now you can check out my gorgeous looks whenever you want."

Amanda carefully masked the fury which was building inside. She fake-smiled and nodded.

"Smile," said Amanda as Roxanne continued to do the duck pose.

The camera flash lit up the room and Roxanne staggered backwards, her vision blurred.

"Oh that's a lovely one," remarked Amanda, as

Roxanne rubbed her eyes.

"Roxanne! Final call!" yelled the woman from the far end of the room, clearly agitated that she'd been made to wait. Roxanne tottered towards the door, struggling to walk in her high-heeled shoes.

Amanda waited. The timing was crucial. She had to hang on until Roxanne was on stage, then she could let the camera do its magic. Amanda listened. She could hear the crowd applaud as Roxanne was introduced. It was show time!

Amanda started with Roxanne's ears. She stretched them on the screen until they were huge and droopy. Next, she quickly began to work on her eyes, widening them so that they looked more like dustbin lids. Finally, she altered her mouth, shrinking it until it was no bigger than a pea!

The screams and howls from the audience began before she could make a start on Roxanne's nose. Amanda peered through a gap at the side of the stage. The last thing she wanted to do was miss the fun.

"Look at her freaky face!" wailed a kid in the front row. Others gasped and covered their mouths. Roxanne stared across at the windows at the side of the hall. She saw her horrifying reflection staring back. An ear-splitting shriek echoed around the hall. Covering her face with her hands, she scampered off stage, her hazardous heels causing her to stagger and sway.

Amanda grinned. But she wasn't so cruel as to leave Roxanne that way forever. She clicked the 'undo' button and the image returned to normal.

The doors flew open and Roxanne appeared like a human whirlwind, still clutching her face and wailing like a banshee. She tottered past Amanda and made for the exit. Before she left, she turned and looked back, removing her hands from her face which had now returned to normal. Roxanne couldn't find any words. She just shook her head in disbelief. Turning around, she barged the doors open and stormed out.

Amanda felt guilty that part one of her plan had been a little cruel, but she was convinced that the means justified the end. Hopefully Roxanne had been taught a lesson she'd never forget. Now it was time for part two of the operation.

Holding up the camera, she clicked a button on the screen and her image appeared on the digital viewfinder. It was time for a selfie. She pushed the button on top of the camera and the bright flash went off. Blinking away the glare, she peered at the screen. One by one, Amanda began to delete the spots on the image.

After erasing all of the spots on her left cheek, she paused as the doors opened. Mum and Dad walked in. Mum looked confused as she noticed the unblemished skin on her daughter's left cheek.

"I think you'd better explain what's going on," said Mum.

Amanda went through the whole episode, pouring her heart out to her parents. She explained what she'd done and how she planned to delete her spots before she went on stage.

Mum and Dad sat either side of their daughter and placed their arms around her.

"You need to learn that in life it doesn't matter what's on the outside. The most important thing is what's on the inside," advised Mum in a tender voice.

"I had awful spots when I was a kid. Some of the other children used to say horrible things. Look at me now though, they've gone," Dad chipped in.

"Looks change as you get older, Amanda, but if you're beautiful on the inside, that will never fade," said Mum, her eyes glistening with tears. "Go out there and show the audience how beautiful you are."

Amanda considered her parents' advice, then clicked the 'undo' button. The spots on her left cheek instantly reappeared. She handed the camera to Dad just as Mrs Green entered the room.

"Sorry about the delay, love. I've no idea what happened. Roxanne's act seemed to go wrong," said Mrs Green. "The audience have calmed down now though. They're ready for you."

Amanda took a deep breath and got to her feet. She followed Mrs Green to the stage. The fact that Amanda sang her heart out and won the top prize seemed irrelevant that night.

From that day on, Mum and Dad's words of wisdom firmly stuck in Amanda's head. She paid a lot less attention to her spots and the occasional jibe which came her way.

As for Roxanne, it appeared that she'd learnt her lesson. She steered well clear of Amanda and never dared to pick on her or any of the other kids ever again.

Mindbender

When I was a kid, I used to suffer from horrific headaches. Now I'm not talking about the sort where you take some medicine and they go away. Or you go to bed for an hour and it disappears. These were far worse. I'm talking booming brain explosions. Imagine a thunderstorm in your head coupled with an erupting volcano and multiply it by ten, then you're getting close to how it felt. They'd happen every couple of months and usually resulted in a day or two off school. Nothing wrong with a couple of days off school, I hear you say. Well there is if your mum's in charge of the school. Mum hated seeing me suffer and she also knew how important my education was, so she wanted to get to the bottom of the problem. After loads of trips to the doctor, who thought I was suffering from migraines, I was sent a hospital appointment.

That's how I ended up flat on my back, waiting for a brain scan.

The radiographers at the hospital were lovely. I wasn't nervous at all. They explained that I was going to slide into a short tunnel. I had to stay very still so that they could take lots of pictures of the inside of my head. It sounded cool and I was quite excited to see what my brain looked like! In fact the whole experience was all a bit of an adventure, if I'm honest.

As the plastic bed I was lying on began to slide into the tube-shaped tunnel, I eagerly waited to see what would happen next. Before long, things got a bit noisy. The radiographer, who was in charge of taking the pictures, had warned me this was going to happen so I didn't panic. Plus I was wearing earplugs so everything was muffled. Apparently that was when the machine was creating the images of my brain. Super cool, hey? After a few minutes, the bed began to move and within a short time, I was out of the machine and back where I'd started, staring up at the ceiling.

"All done. You did a great job," smiled the radiographer. "Go and get dressed. Your mum's waiting outside."

The floor was cold on my bare feet so I hotfooted it to the changing room.

"The results will be through in a few weeks," said Mum over the cubicle wall. "You were ever so brave."

"Ah, it was nothing really. I can't wait to get a look at my brain," I replied, causing Mum to chuckle.

"Fingers crossed they find one in there," she joked, ruffling my hair as I walked out of the cubicle.

Everything felt normal as we got into the car but it turned out that things wouldn't remain that way for long.

* * *

I noticed something weird was happening to me the next day as I was on my way to school. Stopping by the pond, I checked my watch. I was in good time and the sun was streaming down, so I decided to take five minutes on the grass.

As I watched the world go by, I noticed a duck waddling about on the grass. I guessed it was after some food, but unfortunately it wasn't going to get any breakfast from me. My sandwiches were staying in my bag.

I watched as the creature stopped a few metres away and began to quack aggressively. The poor thing must have been starving and it was doing its best to ask for some food.

A stupid thought entered my head. Wouldn't it be funny if the duck could actually talk? I chuckled to myself at the thought of a muttering mallard begging for some grub.

"Alright, mate. Lovely morning, isn't it? Got any bread in that bag of yours? I'm starving."

I looked around. There was nobody else about.

"Oi! Are you deaf or something?"

I looked down at the duck and it was staring directly at me.

"Right, mate, now you're listening, I'll ask again. Have you got any grub?" asked the duck in an aggressive manner.

My mind raced. Ducks can't talk, I thought.

The bird moved closer and began to raucously quack and flap its wings before giving up and waddling off back to the pond.

I grabbed my bag and headed off to school. On the way, I puzzled over what had happened in the park. I'd thought about something completely ridiculous happening, and before my very eyes it had. What on earth was going on?

* * *

At break, I decided to try something. Josh, my best mate, came over and sat down next to me.

"Alright, Isaac. How's things?" he asked.

"Not bad. Keep your eyes on that kid," I replied, pointing at an older, thick-set boy who was crossing the yard. I focused hard and created an image of the kid in my head.

Suddenly, he began to pirouette and prance around like a ballerina. The expression on the kid's face was priceless! His arms were raised above his head and he gracefully teetered on his tiptoes. A group of girls sitting close by began to titter and point. At that moment, I erased the thought of the ballet-dancing kid from my mind and visualised him continuing his walk across the yard.

The poor lad stopped dead. He looked awkward and must have been wondering what had come over him. He shook his head in confusion before hastily dashing off.

"He didn't ever strike me as the dancing type," Josh giggled, his shoulders twitching as he chuckled away. "What was all that about?"

"You wouldn't believe me if I told you," I said.

"Try me," replied Josh, eager to know what was going on.

I explained my brain-scrambling theory as he listened intently, hanging on my every word.

"So you're telling me you can make things happen just by thinking about them?" he whispered.

"I know it sounds mad, but that's exactly what I'm saying," I replied in a hushed tone. "I couldn't do it before I went to the hospital. It's got to be something to do with that scan. That machine's done something amazing to me."

"Sounds cool," Josh squeaked in an excited voice, making me think he was literally about to burst.

"You've got to keep this quiet. I need to work out what's happening first. If word gets out I'll end up being part of a government experiment in a secret underground laboratory," I warned him. I shuddered at the thought of being strapped to a metal table with scientists prodding and probing me, desperate to discover the secret behind my new-found ability.

Josh nodded just as the school bell rang to signal the end of break.

We headed to class and I spent the rest of the day trying hard not to visualise the teachers and pupils in all manner of crazy situations. I was really tempted to make Mrs Mawson, the grumpiest teacher in school, dance around the classroom in the hope of livening up a lesson about deforestation. I just about resisted the temptation. My special ability was a powerful gift and I fully accepted that I still had much to learn about it.

* * *

Mum was late home that evening. When she walked in an aura of stress radiated from her. She immediately started babbling about school. Eventually I was able to understand her ramblings. I found out that she was expecting a visit from some reporters from a magazine.

"They'll be in first thing tomorrow," Mum ranted, as she charged about like a headless chicken. "I need things to go well."

"You'll be fine," I said, trying to calm her. "Lupton Primary's an ace school. I love it there. You're doing a great job. All the teachers are."

Mum's eyes began to fill up. She pulled a tissue from her pocket and dabbed away the tears. "Oh Isaac, that's so lovely. Tomorrow's visit is very important as the reporters will be creating an article about the school. I want to give them a day to remember, so the pressure's on," she explained.

An idea popped into my head. It was a devilishly cunning plan which would allow me to test out my mind-control skills on adults for the first time. It had worked on a duck and a kid but grown-ups were still unknown territory. I pondered whether my powers would be strong enough to control the mind of an adult. My body tingled with excitement at the thought of making grown-ups do whatever I wanted.

I smiled and placed my arms around Mum's waist. I hugged her so tightly I think she feared she might pop. "Everything will be just fine, Mum. Trust me," I reassured her.

Leaving her to deal with a pile of paperwork she was removing from her bag, I went up to my room to think through my plan of action. The next day would be a real test of my mind-controlling ability and I couldn't wait to get started.

* * *

I woke up early the following morning to find sunlight pouring through the wafer-thin curtains. I got dressed, used the bathroom and went downstairs.

Mum was getting her things together, but stopped what she was doing when she spotted me.

"Wish me luck," she said, forcing an anxious smile.

"You'll be great," I reassured her.

She picked up her bag and came over and kissed me on the forehead. After adjusting her hair, she walked out to the car. Then she was gone.

I grabbed breakfast and headed off a little while later. I was excited about the visitors. If my master plan worked out, I'd give Mum a helping hand as well as test the full capabilities of my new-found skill.

* * *

To start the day, the whole school gathered in the hall. Mum nervously paced the stage as three people stood to one side. I didn't recognise them and presumed that they were the reporters.

"Morning," Mum said in a voice which was tinged with nerves. "As you can see, we have some very special visitors joining us today. They've come to see how super our school is."

The two men and a woman stared out across the sea of faces and smiled politely.

Mum began to talk again, but I wasn't listening by this point. It was time to get started.

I stared hard at the tallest man. He had a bald head and a moustache. I closed my eyes and visualised the man in my mind.

Suddenly, he dropped to his knees and began to crawl around the stage on all fours. Mum stopped mid-sentence, her jaw left hanging in the air like the words she'd just spoken. The kids in the hall began to crack up, despite the best efforts of the teachers who were desperately trying to calm them.

Without warning, the man began to bark, sending the packed hall into hysterics. His tongue was hanging from his mouth and he was panting like a thirsty dog. He began to scratch himself like he had fleas, before letting out a high-pitched howl!

"That bloke's barking mad," shouted out a boy at the back of the hall. His mates, who were sitting around him, held their sides and sniggered uncontrollably. Even some of the teachers were doing their best to hold back their laughter. Mr Lyon, my teacher, was biting so hard on his knuckle that it looked like he was going to chew his hand off.

Back on stage, the man had made his way across to the microphone stand next to Mum and was in the process of cocking his leg next to it. The children roared with laughter but that was the final straw for his two colleagues. They dashed over and hauled him to his feet. At that point, I closed my eyes and visualised the man as he'd originally been, standing on the stage with a blank expression on his face.

The baffled bloke didn't know what to do or how to react. He stared vacantly as he was supported by his colleagues, one on either side. I could see him mouthing to one of them. "I don't know what came over me," he was repeating over and over.

"He needs to go home. He's clearly not well," said the woman as they ushered out the befuddled man.

They guided him from the stage as Mum tried to bring a close to the chaotic scenes by instructing everyone to return to class. The hall quickly emptied.

As I walked out, I marvelled at what had just taken place. My powers were strong and I'd proved they could control an adult's behaviour, but was that a fluke? Another test was required.

* * *

After biding my time until lunch, I headed to the canteen. I scanned the room and spotted the two remaining visitors with Mum. There was a free seat opposite them, so I hurried over and sat down, smiling sweetly. As I began to eat my lunch, they asked me lots of questions. Mum nervously watched, silently praying that I'd give the right answers.

As I tucked into my sandwich, I focused on the woman. I concentrated intently and pictured her in my mind's eye.

Suddenly, she raised both her fists and slammed them down on the table, making the cups and plates jump and clatter. She then screwed up her face into a scrunched-up ball and began to wail like a badly behaved toddler.

"Me not like this food," she yelled in a little kid's voice, flinging the plate across the table. The dinner hall fell silent. All eyes were on the developing scene and after the earlier show, nobody wanted to miss a second of the unfolding action.

The woman then grabbed her cup and launched it across the hall. It rebounded off the wall, narrowly missing a kid who was eating a slice of pizza, and landed on the floor. The chaos escalated to a new level as the raging woman pushed her chair back and threw herself to the floor where she hollered and screamed. Her fists flailed as she kicked her feet wildly in all directions. She was throwing the toddler tantrum of the century, and it was just how I was imagining it in my head.

Keen to get the woman away from the gathered audience, who stared in disbelief, Mum and the man tried to pick her up. She lashed out viciously with her arms and let out an ear-piercing scream. Veins bulged in her neck and her face was bright red. She was going berserk and appeared completely out of control!

Mum and the man grabbed an arm each and dragged the woman out of the hall. She slid along the polished tiles, kicking and screaming every inch of the way before she disappeared out of the double doors at the rear of the hall. Only at that point did her screams begin to fade.

I didn't see the woman again that day. I found out later from Mum that she'd been sent home to rest up until she felt better.

I smiled broadly to myself as I tidied away the rubbish into my lunchbox. Things were going perfectly.

* * *

The final step of the operation required accurate timing. Mum had said that she was due to meet with the magazine reporters just before the end of the day.

I'd been watching the clock closely and there were only fifteen minutes until the end of school. As I turned to look out of the window, I spotted the remaining visitor walking across the yard, chatting away to Mum.

I raised my hand and lied to Mr Lyon that I needed the toilet. He allowed me to leave class. Rather than visiting the toilets though, I made my way down the corridor towards Mum's office.

As I turned the corner I could hear Mum's voice, so I dived into the cloakroom, hiding among the coats. Peering out between a duffle coat and a parka, I watched as Mum opened her office door and waited until they had walked in.

After making sure the coast was clear, I crossed the corridor and, standing on my tiptoes, peered through the window. The man was sitting at Mum's desk drinking from a plastic cup. She was looking intently at him, awaiting his verdict on what must have been the craziest day he'd ever experienced. I'd had my fun for the day and now it was time for the final part of my mind-controlling master plan. It was crucial that things went smoothly.

Just as I was about to close my eyes and let my thoughts go to work, the man started to talk. I hurriedly cleared my mind and listened carefully.

"I know we've had a couple of bizarre events today, but I must compliment your pupils on the sensible way they dealt with them. We've seen so many great things going on in your school – you're doing a brilliant job here at Lupton," he said. "Your pupils all seem happy, which is marvellous to see. Well done to you and your staff, Mrs Wilson. I can't wait to put together the article which will showcase your amazing school. One thing is for sure, I won't mention the two unfortunate incidents. The less said about those the better."

Mum thanked the man and smiled broadly. They continued to chat and it was lovely to see her grinning from ear to ear.

I'd seen enough to realise that my mind powers wouldn't be required for a third time that day. My heart sang as I watched Mum beam with pride. As I'd reassured her that morning, everything had turned out just fine.

The clock in the office was showing two minutes until the end of school, so I realised it was time to make a sharp exit. The final bell of the day rang not long after I'd arrived back in class. I made my way home to await Mum's arrival.

I'll never forget the look of delight on Mum's face when she got in; it was a total contrast to the previous evening. She explained, with great pride, what had been said and I did my best to pretend it was the first time I'd heard it. Everything had worked out and we celebrated with a hug.

I was tempted to tell Mum about the mind tricks I'd played that day, but I felt it was best to keep quiet for a variety of reasons. Plus, I was only just getting started. Just imagine what I'd be capable of doing with some more practice.

Acknowledgements

Firstly, I'd like to thank Dad for his ongoing support and listening ear. His advice is always valued and often called upon. As always, I'm sad that Mum didn't get to read my stories, but I know that when I'm struggling with something, only for the solution to appear out of nowhere, the chances are it's down to my mum helping me out from afar.

It was great to have the super-talented Martin Spore involved again. His illustrative and design skills are simply amazing. I love the book cover and the story title illustrations.

I would also like to extend my appreciation to Kevin Barber, who has done a fantastic job with the formatting and layout of the book interior. I'm sure you'll agree that it looks fab.

Yet again, Clare O'Malley proved to be a reliable source of support and reassurance. She listened to the Tales as they were taking shape, even though the cow poo and snot themes made her stomach flip!

When the stories are coming together, it's so important for me to get fresh eyes on them. I'd like to thank Judy Earnshaw, Jackie Simpson and Phil Whiteley for reading the Tales in the early stages and providing me with lots of constructive feedback.

I was thrilled to bits when Sandra Mangan agreed

to edit the Tales. Sandra has been involved in all of my writing projects. Yet again, she did a great job of editing my writing, and further down the line, proofing the book.

Thank you to Lesley Bennett, Barbara Strachan, Val Hall, Carol Cowling, Alexis Filby, Claire Andrews, Sharon Bowie, the Spore family and the Russel family for taking the time to read through the proof copies.

There are many other people who have supported me during the process of writing the Tales. They know who they are and I appreciate what each and every one of them has done.

A Note From The Author

Thanks so much for reading the Tales, I hope you enjoyed them as much as I enjoyed creating and writing them. It proved quite a challenge to write eight new short stories but I loved every minute of the process right from the first ideas through to the final stories.

Fingers crossed you might be able to create your own Impossible Tale now that you've read mine. I start off with an object or idea from a real-life situation then I puzzle over what could happen. The wackier and weirder the better! That's how the Tales start life. Have a go and see what you can create.

Reading is such a cool thing to do and it helps you so much with your writing. I read loads of books and I always encourage the children I meet to find a book and get reading. It doesn't matter where you get your books from – just grab a book and get reading!

My next book will see the return of Eric Appleby. Keep your eyes peeled for his new story as another action-packed adventure awaits young Eric. Until next time, keep reading and work hard on your writing. See you again soon.

Website: www.danworsley.com
Twitter: @dan__worsley

47983937R00073

Printed in Poland
by Amazon Fulfillment
Poland Sp. z o.o., Wrocław